"Jesus," Longarm

The dead men had not merely been shot.

They had been shot to pieces.

Quite literally to pieces. The worst of them was held together at the extremities only by tattered scraps of flesh. The best of them was missing most of his head.

Their deaths had been as good as murder.

Then, inexplicably, the group of nervous peons scattered, all of them turning almost in a single motion and racing away into the fields, leaving their dead and wounded behind as they dashed off with loud cries of fear and warning.

Longarm looked back the way the men had been staring as they fled.

Eight riders were approaching along the river bank. Eight men carrying Winchester carbines in their hands.

Longarm's fingers moved involuntarily to touch the butt of his Colt . . .

BOOKS 'N' THINGS
1411 1st AVE. S.W.
AUSTIN, MN 55912
507-437-2592

TABOR EVANS

LONGARM

AND THE BLOOD HARVEST

JOVE BOOKS, NEW YORK

LONGARM AND THE BLOOD HARVEST

A Jove Book/published by arrangement with
the author

PRINTING HISTORY
Jove edition/December 1987

All rights reserved.
Copyright © 1987 by Jove Publications, Inc.
This book may not be reproduced in whole or in part,
by mimeograph or any other means, without permission.
For information address: The Berkley Publishing Group,
200 Madison Avenue, New York, New York 10016.

ISBN: 0-515-09325-4

Jove Books are published by The Berkley Publishing Group,
200 Madison Avenue, New York, New York 10016.
The name "JOVE" and the "J" logo
are trademarks belonging to Jove Publications, Inc.

PRINTED IN THE UNITED STATES OF AMERICA

10 9 8 7 6 5 4 3 2 1

Chapter 1

It was a fine day, the kind of day that makes a man want to puff out his chest, suck in his belly, and breathe deep.

Deputy U.S. Marshal Custis Long did exactly that. He stopped on the top step at the entrance to the Federal Building and stood there for a moment simply enjoying the feel of the morning air and the sharp, pleasantly biting scent of smoke from countless breakfast fires. Denver's Colfax Avenue was busy this morning. Hansom cabs and handsome coaches plied back and forth, carrying men on their way to business meetings and ladies to the shops.

A particularly fetching red-haired miss rolled past in the company of her very nearly as attractive mother. Her eyes swept over Longarm as their coach neared the imposing gray stone building, hesitated only for a moment and then cut back toward him while she pretended to examine something behind him.

Longarm removed the cheroot from between his teeth and smiled, exposing white teeth in a deeply tanned face surrounded by brown to complement the tan. Brown, sweeping moustache, brown hair, and brown Stetson. His tweed coat and corduroy trousers were in shades of brown as well. The only accents of black on him were his tall stovepipe boots and the gunbelt that rode at his waist.

He smiled and the girl looked quickly away, blushing enough to make her mother notice. The older woman leaned forward and said something, obviously a rebuke, that made the girl blush even more and turn her pretty face toward the other side of the street.

Then the mama startled Longarm and possibly herself as

well. When the girl was looking elsewhere, the woman gave Longarm a quick and frankly appreciative inspection of her own, and followed it with a smiling wink.

Longarm laughed and watched the two of them pass out of sight toward the gold-domed state capitol building and the shopping districts nearby.

It was that kind of delightful morning, he thought, when absolutely nothing could go wrong.

He pulled his watch from his vest pocket and glanced at it. He was not even very late this morning. Just a few minutes, which for him was practically early. He returned the watch to his pocket and took another pull on the cheroot. Just another minute to finish his smoke and enjoy the morning, then he would go inside.

"Long!" The voice came from behind him, from the front doors of the massive building. It was sharp and irritating.

Longarm took his time about responding, exhaling slowly and examining the damp, half-chewed end of the cheroot before he turned to see who could be mad at him so early in the day. It wasn't Billy Vail. He already knew that. The United States Marshal for the Denver District was not in the habit of chewing on his men in public even when they needed it, and as far as Longarm knew he should be in Billy's good graces anyway for the work he had been doing lately.

"Long!" the slightly nasal voice came at him again.

The speaker approached him and grabbed his sleeve from behind.

Longarm stiffened and turned to give the man a chill glare of warning. He thought he recognized that voice now, and he was right. Pity about that. He could have gone all month without running into this red-tape-wrapped asshole and not minded it.

The man saw the ice in Longarm's eyes and the hostility in the set of his jaw and turned loose of Longarm's sleeve like the cloth had suddenly burst into flame.

The man took half a step backward, then recovered his aplomb and set his own jaw. "You're late," he accused.

Longarm took his time about replacing the cheroot between his teeth and taking a puff before he answered. Deliberately he let the smoke trickle out toward the smaller man's nostrils when he spoke. Dalton Foster hated the smell of cigar smoke. "Go report me to somebody then, Foster. Give you something to do today. You can get your secretary to write up four copies of it on that fancy machine. It'll give her something to do today too."

Foster's secretary was a woman—a rarity in government offices—and most attractive. Longarm happened to know that the clerks who gathered in the musty back of the file room for their coffee spent much of their time trying to figure out whether the girl ever actually performed any work in exchange for the government paycheck she drew. The rest of the time they spent envying Dalton Foster the afternoon hours he and the secretary spent behind a closed and locked office door.

"I don't like your innuendo, Long."

Foster huffed and puffed and tried to look threatening, but he just wasn't built for it. He was a head shorter than Longarm and scrawny to boot. He dressed in expensive suits and affected a gold-headed malacca whenever he was away from his office. Longarm suspected that if Foster had had the cane in his hand at the moment he might have tried to hit the tall deputy with it.

"Don't take on so, Foster. You'll get the apoplexy and fall over sideways." He exhaled smoke in Foster's direction again and pretended a close inspection of the man's impeccably barbered features. "Besides, Dalton, you oughta be happy today. I think your acne's finally clearing up." Foster was at least in his late thirties but he had been cursed with a face that probably would make him look sixteen until he died of old age. That was one of many things he was sensitive about.

The young-looking face twisted and darkened with rage. "You son of a bitch," he hissed.

"There you go, Foster. Apoplexy for sure. I told you I could see it coming. Want me to find a doctor for you? Or should I just squeeze that big pimple on top of your neck and put you out of your misery." Longarm grinned and tossed the stub of the cheroot away. "If you'll excuse me now, Foster, I got to get to work." He stepped around the little man.

Foster stopped him before he got a hand on the door pull by saying, "Damn right you'll get to work now, Long. And on time from now on. As long as you are working for me, that is."

Longarm turned and fixed a cold stare on the little bastard again, but this time Foster did not back down. This time he returned it. And Dalton Foster's look was one of triumphant satisfaction.

"That's right, damn you," Foster said, not even attempting to keep the note of spite from his voice. "You're working for me now, Long. And *this* time you'll be doing things by the book."

The chill that had been in Longarm's eyes sank to a new and unwelcome location—his belly.

He was going to have to work under this grade-A governmental asshole? He would hand Billy his badge before that ever came to pass.

"We'll see about that," he snarled, and headed inside.

Behind him he could hear Dalton Foster's wicked laughter follow him down the hall and on toward the Justice Department offices.

Longarm stomped into Billy Vail's office, pulled out his wallet, and threw it down in front of the startled marshal.

"What the—?"

"Badge, wallet, the whole heap. You can have it all."

Vail puffed out his cheeks, rolled his eyes, and exhaled slowly. He leaned back in his chair, ignoring for the moment the piles of official papers strung out across the surface of his desk, and motioned his top deputy toward a seat. "I take it you've seen Dalton Foster this morning." It wasn't really a question.

"Billy, you *know* how I feel about that son of a bitch," Longarm began.

Vail waved him into silence but took another moment to gather his thoughts before he spoke.

It was not exactly a secret, not in this office nor upstairs in the Bureau of Indian Affairs, about the past difficulties between Deputy Marshal Custis Long and Superintendent Dalton Foster.

The two had clashed several times, one of those times quite seriously. The way Longarm saw it, Foster was a political hack, an appointee of the worst sort who curried favor with his superiors and felt neither compassion nor any sense of obligation toward the Indian Americans who were supposed to be the wards of his branch of government. He could recite rules and regulations by rote but he cared nothing about the effect those rules would have when applied to human beings. The way Foster undoubtedly saw it, Long was a maverick—or worse—who flaunted rules, defied orders, and should long ago have been fired from government service.

The last time the two men had been working the same ground, Foster's blind adherence to a rule book written in Washington by men who had likely never seen a live Indian—at least none outside one of the Wild West shows—very nearly precipitated a bloody, three-sided war among the Sioux, the Pawnee, and the United States Army. And all over the meaningless question of whether every tribe should be allowed to slaughter its own issue beeves with its own horses and spears or if the reservation agent in charge of each tribe or tribal branch had the right to enforce his preferences in the matter and arbitrarily require the establishment of sanitary, approved butcher shops on reservation lands. Longarm had found the whole question ignorant. And Dalton Foster too.

Persuading the Sioux to bend just a bit had been no problem at all. But getting the BIA to accept a Sioux interpretation of the regulations—which an officer named Long just might have suggested to them—was a bitch. Longarm was convinced that Foster would rather see a full-blown war than wink at a rule. Yet the whole thing had been so simple, really. The Sioux appointed their own "inspector" to oversee the butchering . . . and to certify that the conditions of slaughter were sanitary and appropriate under tribal laws. The BIA regulation had not, after all, said who the inspector had to be, only that there must be one. And the regulations hadn't exactly defined "sanitary," either,

5

just that the conditions should be so. Simple. But to get that across and avoid conflict with the Sioux, who were not being allowed to slaughter their own beeves, and the Pawnee, who were, and the army, which had been called in by a panicky Foster, Longarm had had to go over Foster's head with a direct appeal to the chief of Foster's department.

The hostility between the two men had become damn near legendary in the halls of the Federal Building since then.

And Billy Vail knew that every bit as well as anybody.

"Let me try to explain this, Longarm," Vail said mildly.

Longarm started to protest, but Billy cut him off again. "Please. Just hear me out. Will you do that for me? Listen to what I have to say. Then, if you refuse the assignment, I won't try to force you to take it. And you certainly don't have to resign over it." He flipped Longarm's wallet closed and tossed it back to him with a smile.

Longarm snorted with disgust, but he returned the wallet to his pocket and sat where Billy wanted him to.

Unlike Foster, Billy Vail was *not* just a political hack. He was a fine peace officer in his own right and a good man to work with as well as for. Longarm owed him time to explain, he grudgingly admitted.

"All right, Billy. But if you think I'm gonna work with that son of a bitch—"

"I know. Just listen. That's all I'm asking, Longarm. Just listen to why I'd ask this of you. Then make up your own mind."

Longarm sniffed unhappily but kept his mouth shut, even though he was beginning to get the feeling that listening was going to be a mistake. Mild-looking, balding Billy could be persuasive when he wanted. And he had to have something up his sleeve, damn him, or he wouldn't have been so willing to leave the decision to Longarm. Longarm suspected he was being suckered somehow, but he had said he would listen, so listen he would.

Not that he was going to change his mind about it, of course. He would just sit here polite and quiet and hear

6

Billy out. Then he would tell Billy to shove the job up Dalton Foster's backside.

With a grunt that clearly said his mind was closed even if his ears were open, Longarm folded his arms and sat back in the seat to do his duty to Billy Vail and to the badge they both carried.

The story Vail laid out for him was an all-too-common one. A tribe of Indians—in this case the Zuni in western New Mexico Territory—were in conflict with a neighboring group of whites over irrigation rights.

The identity of the Indian tribe was something of a surprise, of course. Unlike most tribes, whose members were used to a hunting way of life and who had no concept of land ownership, the Zunis were a pueblo tribe, farmers for longer than they had a history, and had their own established rules of freehold that blended almost perfectly with the white concepts of real property ownership.

Moreover, the Zunis had lived peacefully with their neighbors, white and Mexican and Indian alike, for two centuries, ever since some of them participated in a dust-up with the Spanish back in the 1600s, if Longarm was remembering correctly. If they'd been able to get along with the folks next door that long, he figured, they could be expected to keep it up for a bit longer.

Yet what Billy told him was that the peace was about to be shattered.

"They ain't fighters," Longarm injected at one point.

"No, and they aren't stupid either. They know they haven't much chance of turning themselves into warriors overnight. But they've adapted rather well in some ways. They farm, and they have surplus crops to sell. Therefore they have cash to work with. Word has it that some of them have been gathering funds for the purchase of arms . . ."

"And the hiring of trainers too, Billy? Hell, if they had all the rifles from the Springfield Armory, they couldn't—"

"Will you hear me out? You said you would."

"Sorry."

"As I was about to say, Longarm, the Zuni are peaceful but not ignorant. They understand their own limitations.

7

They can't mount an army overnight no matter how well they arm themselves. What they are thinking about doing . . . what they are on the verge of doing if they aren't stopped . . . is buying arms and deliberately turning them over to their neighbors to the west."

Longarm's brow wrinkled. "To the west. That'd be the Apache. But the Apache aren't at war with anybody right now that I've heard of."

"Right now they aren't." Billy left his desk and went to the sideboard. "Drink?"

"Isn't it a little early for that?"

"I didn't know you ever found it too early for that."

Longarm grunted. Billy was up to something here. He wanted to give him a moment to chew on that last bit, he figured. That business at the sideboard had nothing to do with an offer of a drink. Bully didn't drink at this hour, and he also didn't stock anything in the office that Custis Long would want.

"The Apache are quiet right now," Longarm said stubbornly.

"Uh-huh. So they are. And you believe they would stay that way if someone offered to finance a shipment of breech-loading rifles and a mountain of ammunition, free for nothing?"

Longarm sighed. The Apache—Nadene, really—weren't so much a tribe as a whole bunch of individuals who all spoke the same language. Most Indian tribes were pretty much like that, a fact that whites never seemed to understand, the concepts of government between the two being so different. Whites tended to think that the chief of an Indian tribe could declare a war or call a truce pretty much the way the president of the United States could, and that just wasn't so. Indian chiefs didn't rule, they led. And the only other Indians they were leading at any given moment were the ones who chose to go along. And even those might change their minds in ten minutes and go do something else. The Nadene, now, they were more independent-minded than most Indian tribes, even. And there were always a whole bunch of young Nadene anxious to get in

8

on the glory and the booty to be had in a good old shooting war.

If somebody dumped a load of modern guns in their laps it would be like setting fire to a powder keg. Jump back, boys, 'cause something's gonna go.

"I think I have your attention," Vail observed after watching Longarm work through it all.

"Yeah."

"I'm asking you to do this, Longarm, for several reasons. One is that the Apache, if it comes to that and Lord knows I hope it doesn't, but if it does, Longarm, the Apache already know and trust you."

"I don't know as I'd go that far."

Vail shrugged. "Closer to it than anyone else in this department can come, anyway, and a damn sight closer than anyone in the BIA ever will come."

"I s'pose," Longarm said, although he bitterly hated to admit it right at this moment.

"The Zuni have heard about you too."

"But I've never—"

"I know, but information like that seems to travel. They've heard about you from somewhere, maybe from the Apache, the Kiowa-Apache, I really don't know. The fact remains, when they heard the Justice Department would be sending someone to investigate, they specifically asked for you."

"I bet that caused a lot of smiles upstairs," Longarm said, thinking of Foster and his underlings.

"As a matter of fact, and this surprised me too when I learned who the BIA had in charge of their end of it, they endorse the request. You have had successful and much friendlier dealings with some of their personnel in the past."

"But old Foster is handling it for the BIA, and he didn't beef?"

Vail frowned. "Superintendent Foster is representing the Bureau of Indian Affairs, yes, and he made no objection to your assignment. In fact, he added his personal endorsement to the request. I took the liberty of discussing it with him, Longarm. He said it was for the good of the Zuni, the

9

Apache, and the government, and that any personal differences should be laid aside for the time being."

"He didn't act like that outside, Billy. He acted like he thought he had me right under his thumb with this one."

Billy gave Longarm an innocent smile and spread his hands. "Tell me something, Longarm. Does the fact that Superintendent Foster believes something to be true *make* that something true?"

"Not damn likely," Longarm said with a snort.

Billy's smile became a grin.

"You're saying you'd really like me to help with this case but that I don't have to take any bullshit from him while I'm doing it."

"Now, Custis, you know I *always* advocate complete cooperation between agencies. But I do hope you'll keep in mind that you work for me, the Attorney General, and the President of these United States. In that precise order. And I don't expect any of the three of us to be in New Mexico Territory any time this month."

Longarm cleared his throat and squirmed on the hard seat of the chair Billy had pointed him to. Most anybody could probably get along with the Zuni to handle that part of it. But if it came to working with the Apache, well, it wasn't any horn-blowing to admit that he had a better chance than anybody else of heading off something like that.

Billy was right about something else too. Foster could think what he liked; it wouldn't make a lick of difference in the way Custis Long did his job.

Hell, Longarm thought, if he knew old Foster, the bastard would hole up in the plushest hotel in Gallup, anyhow, so he could stay comfortable while he issued orders. He likely wouldn't be anywhere near the Zuni pueblo until everything was smoothed out and it was time for somebody to take credit. Then, of course, he'd be there with bells on.

If this business wasn't taken care of by somebody, there could be a lot of folks killed. For sure there would be if Foster tried to tend to it himself. Maybe Longarm could stop that from happening in spite of the idiot.

Longarm grunted again and squirmed some more. "Give

me the damn file, Billy. I'll read it before I head for the train station. Damn you."

Billy Vail was gracious enough to refrain from rubbing it in. He kept a straight face as he handed the folder across the desk to his best deputy.

Chapter 2

Longarm frowned and shook his head. He took a deep breath and tried again. "Look, it's a simple enough request. I want to get to Gallup. That's in New Mexico. West side o' the territory. You know. New Mexico?"

The ticket agent looked every bit as exasperated as Longarm felt. "I'm trying to accommodate you, Marshal. Truly I am." The man in the sleeve garters and green eye-shade thumped a fingertip on the rather grubby white sheets of the book laid open on the counter between them. "Truly, Marshal, you are being unreasonable. We haven't even got all our track laid yet in this country, much less having connections down into Mexico. A year, maybe two—"

"*New* Mexico," Longarm said again, mustering all the patience he possessed and then some. "Not Mexico. *New* Mexico. It's a territory of the United States of America. You must've heard of it."

"Yeah, sure." The clerk sounded neither convincing nor particularly interested. Mexico and New Mexico seemed quite the same to him. "Point is, Marshal, we got no track laid that far, wherever the hell it is."

"Let's try another approach," Longarm said, as much to himself as to the ticket agent. "I need to get down to the Four Corners country. Mancos?" The clerk continued to look blank. "Durango, Colorado?"

The clerk smiled. Maybe they were getting somewhere.

"I could get you to Silverton. We have track there and stage connections south. Track partway to Durango, I think."

Longarm debated which way to go. This line would take

13

him over the bulk of the mountains and part of the way south. The D&RG would take him south but not west. Either way, it was going to be difficult getting there.

He sighed. It was kind of like the old saw about that farmer who gave up trying to give directions to the stranger and stormed off saying, "Mister, you just cain't get there from here."

There was a tug on his coat sleeve. He turned to see a round-faced young messenger who earned a little money running errands around the Federal Building. Longarm recognized the kid immediately, but it took him a moment to dredge the boy's name out of his memory. "Hello, Tommy."

The boy was panting like he'd run the whole way from the office rather than spending money for a ride. "Glad I caughtcha, Mr. Long." He paused to get his breath. "Message, sir. From Mr. Foster."

Longarm raised an eyebrow.

"You're t'... you're t' meet him, sir. 'S'afternoon. Three o'clock. His office. Something 'bout trip y'all are takin' together?" The boy sounded politely incredulous. As well he might. It was hardly a secret what Longarm and Foster thought about each other.

"A trip we're taking together?" That was damn sure news to Longarm.

"That's what he said, Mr. Long. You're t' meet... him at three... an' get your orders."

Longarm smiled and draped an arm over the young man's shoulders. "Why don't you call me Longarm, Tommy? And, here. Let's you and me go over to the lunch counter and get you something while you rest up."

"I don't know as I should do that, Mis... uh, Longarm. Mr. Foster said I was to check every rail depot in town an' find you before you got off, 'cause he needs t' see you before you leave so you and him—"

"Oh, I think we'll worry about that later. What would you like, Tommy? Cocoa? Lots of energy in cocoa. And how about one of those crullers? They look fresh." He motioned the counter man closer. "Bring my young friend here whatever he wants. My treat, Tommy." Longarm reached into his pocket for some coins, and the young messenger grinned.

"Now the thing is, Tommy," Longarm went on blithely, "it wouldn't be your fault if I'd already boarded that train over there before you could find me, would it?"

Tommy's eyes widened. He might have said something, but his mouth was full of gooey pastry already, and the counter man was placing a steaming cup of cocoa in front of him.

"No need for ol' Fisheye to know different," Longarm said with a grin. The nickname given to Dalton Foster was generally reserved for use in the file-room gossip sessions, and Longarm probably was not supposed to be privy to it. Tommy snorted a bit, spraying crumbs onto the counter.

The kid swallowed hurriedly and grinned. "I don't know if I oughta do that, Longarm. You know how Fisheye is. Why, he'd—"

"Sure he would," Longarm agreed quickly. "If he knew about it." He winked at the messenger boy and rang a quarter onto the counter to pay for the pastry and cocoa.

Tommy chuckled. "Sure is a shame I wasn't in time."

"There'll be change from that quarter, Tommy. You keep it. Me, I gotta go catch that train before it pulls out."

Out on the loading platform the conductor was already tilting the steel steps into the coaches to prepare for departure.

"See you, Tommy." Longarm picked up his gear and headed outside to the platform. There was no need to bother the ticket agent again. His government rail pass would serve after he got aboard.

And there was no need either to fret about which route he should take to get down to New Mexico. This one that was handy and leaving right now was definitely the one to pick.

The narrow-gauge steam engine had already begun applying power to the driving wheels before Longarm tossed his carpetbag and saddle through the door of a passenger coach and pulled himself into the car.

Tommy grinned at him and waved goodbye as Longarm disappeared inside the coach. The kid's mouth was still

15

full, and he was reaching for another cruller the last Long-arm saw of him.

Longarm climbed down from the creaking, squeaky-wheeled coach and unloaded his things from the luggage boot at the rear of the old rig. The stagecoach was a fit match for Gallup; both of them were small and sun-baked and drab. But he had gotten here, difficult though it had been to make the many necessary connections.

He bit off the tip of a cheroot, lighted the smoke, and left it stuck in his jaw at a jaunty angle. "Thanks," he told the driver.

"Any time." The driver unhooked the traces from his sweating team and led the horses forward. The company hostler had not yet appeared with the fresh team that should have been waiting.

"I don't suppose you could tell me where I could hire a saddle horse."

"Mister, I don't know nothing about this town except how t' get out of it again. Change the team, transfer the mail, and I'm gone."

"Thanks anyway, then."

"Any time," the driver repeated. The hostler appeared with the fresh drafters, and the driver was concentrating on them, inspecting them with practiced ease and already bawling out the hostler for not having enough medicine on a harness gall that had developed on one of the new wheelers.

Longarm turned away and carried his gear with him down the dusty main street. He had been the only incoming passenger, and no crowd had gathered to meet the stage. A few Navajo stood nearby pretending disinterest but missing nothing. Longarm nodded to them and headed for the near-est saloon. A drink would be good to cut the dust of the coach trip, and he could get the information he wanted there quite as well as anywhere else.

"Rye whiskey," he said. "Maryland distilled if you've got it." He laid a dime on the bar.

"No rye," the barkeep said. "Bar whiskey or beer, that's all I got."

"A beer, then." He knew better than to trust the bar

16

whiskey in a place like this one. It would be raw alcohol diluted with whatever came to hand, and too many saloon owners had too good a sense of humor when it came to what they sold to a thirsty public. "And some information."

Instead of making change from the dime, the barman set two mugs of frothy beer in front of Longarm and dropped the coin into his apron pocket before he propped his elbows on the bar. "What information can I give you?"

"I need to hire a horse, and I'll need directions down to Zuni Pueblo," Longarm said.

"The directions are easy enough. Y' take the only road south an' keep to the main road till you get there. As for hiring the horse, you'll likely wait till tomorra."

"You don't have a livery in town?"

"Now that ain't exactly what I said. Said you'll have to wait till tomorra. This afternoon most everything's closed down for the funeral. That's where most everybody is right now. Later on they'll stop here for the wake. But as many bottles as went outa here this morning, I don't expect too many places'll reopen this afternoon."

"Funeral?"

"Got you a hearing problem, mister? I can speak up if you want."

Longarm smiled at him. "Sorry. I just got in. I think my brain's still about ten miles out of town and bouncing up and down on that road."

"Yeah, well, it gets like that. Best thing for you t' do would be to take a room for the night an' talk to d'Angelis, he's the man runs the livery, come morning. Not too early in the morning, though. He won't want t' do any business till his head stops pounding."

"Sounds like a helluva deal, this funeral and wake."

"Should be. Big man like Wilse Howard gets himself killed, there's gonna be a lot o' celebrating going on."

"Not grieving," Longarm observed. "Celebrating."

"You're feelin' better already, I see. Hearing clearin' up an' everything."

"Yeah, and some curious too," Longarm agreed.

The bartender shrugged. It was obvious he hadn't anything better to do than to chat. The only other customer in the place at the moment was passed out at a table. "Like I said, a big man like that gets himself killed, there's winks and celebration and not too many questions asked."

"This Howard fella was the he-coon of the country, then?"

"Aye. He thought so, anyhow. Owned the bank an' about half of everything else around here. Foreclosed on a lot o' folks while he could. Now all them folks are thinking things could get easier with him gone."

"How'd the man die?" Longarm finished the first beer and started on the second. The quality of this man's whiskey might be in doubt, but there was nothing wrong with his beer.

The bartender grinned. "Nobody knows, exactly. Old Wilse was setting at his desk, prob'ly counting his notes due or somethin' like that, an' some civic-minded soul outside . . . it was night, y' understand . . . somebody outside put a bullet through the window. Stray shot let off by accident, everybody figures. Took old Wilse plumb in the side of the head and ruint a lot of the mortgage papers where he bled on 'em. Can't read a word on them papers, they're saying. Nobody's fault, though, the whole thing being an accident like that." The barman smiled happily enough that Longarm suspected his had been one of those supposedly now illegible notes.

"And the law here accepts the idea that it was an accidental gunshot?"

"Sure. Had us a coroner's jury assembled just this morning for an inquest. It's all ruled an' written down as official as you please. Accidental as hell."

Longarm took another swallow of beer. Perhaps the stuff was not quite as good as he had thought.

Not that the rulings of some local coroner's inquest were of any interest to him. Certainly not officially. There were a great many things that were against federal law, but murder was not one of them unless the victim was a federal employee or a ward of the government. It did, however, tell him something about the quality of the local law that he might find himself working with on this case.

18

Gallup was the nearest seat of civilian territorial government and the BIA's headquarters in the area as well. If he had to deal with civilian authorities, this was where he would have to do it. And it was looking like their interests were keyed strongly to local opinion and the hell with inconsequentials like justice or the questions of right versus wrong.

Interesting, but probably not important, Longarm thought. He finished his beer and thanked the barman for the information.

"My pleasure," the bartender said. "Hotel's in the next block down an' across the street," he volunteered. "The livery, when you need it, is at the other end o' town and a block over."

"Thanks again." Longarm picked up his things and went out into the sunglare of the street.

Since it looked like he would have some time to kill here, he might as well get a room and then make a call at the BIA district headquarters before supper. He tossed the stub of his cheroot into the street and headed toward the hotel, conscious of dark eyes following his progress as the Indians, who were the only people visible in Gallup at the moment, watched while pretending not to.

Chapter 3

"My gracious, Marshal Long, I'm certainly glad you chose to stop here before going on. Your department..." He clucked his tongue and fluttered his hands and shook his head. "Really quite inefficient, you know. Shoddy briefing as to the situation here, if I do say so, although of course I mean nothing *personal* about it. Not your fault, I am sure. But still..." Whitson clucked and tutted and fluttered some more.

Longarm kept his expression impassive and did not bother trying to correct this bureaucrat's opinion about the alleged failings of the Justice Department. But Longarm had certain ideas of his own about who might be responsible for the incomplete briefing. And it wasn't Billy Vail that he was thinking of. Dalton Foster would like nothing better than for Custis Long to come down here and make an ass of himself, preferably in such a way that the errors would show up when official reports were filed.

The first bit of misinformation had been apparent as soon as Longarm walked in the door of the BIA office and asked who he should see at Zuni Pueblo about their irrigation problems.

It turned out there was no on-site agent at Zuni Pueblo to look out for the Zuni interests.

"There is no need for that," Whitson had said. "The Zuni are peaceful and quite self-sufficient for the most part. It would be a waste of taxpayer funds to establish an agency there. No need for it, you see. I handle the Zuni myself, as the need arises, in addition to my regular duties as district agent overseeing the reservation agencies for the Navajo, the Jicarilla, and a small reservation given to the

21

Utes. Generally speaking, though, there is little need for direct involvement with the Zuni."

"Then why. . .?"

"And to begin with, Marshal, your task here . . . and, mind you, sir, I do not oppose your presence here, quite the contrary . . . your task here has nothing to do with Zuni Pueblo."

That certainly got Longarm's attention. If there was no problem at Zuni Pueblo, what in hell was he doing here?

"No, indeed," Whitson went on with a fluttery gesture. "The land immediately surrounding Zuni Pueblo is reservation land, you see. No jurisdictional problems with that whatsoever. No, the current difficulty lies at Vega Zuni."

"Never heard of it," Longarm said bluntly.

"Vega Zuni is one of the satellite pueblos. Quite small and not nearly so old as Zuni Pueblo itself." Whitson left his desk and went to a file cabinet, where he began shuffling through some folders, talking over his shoulder while he searched for whatever it was he wanted. "Vega Zuni, you see, is located on a stream called Rio de las Vegas, which is a tributary of Rio Zuni."

Longarm grunted. He'd never heard of that either.

"Southeast from here. Northeast of Zuni Pueblo. Many of the pueblo dwelling tribes established outlying pueblos —suburb communities, so to speak—around them during times of population increase during the old days. Ah, yes, here is the file." He carefully marked the place the file was taken from and closed the drawer before returning to the desk and resuming his seat.

"Yes, um, Vega Zuni. We currently list twenty-three Zuni families resident at Vega Zuni." Apparently that exciting bit of information was what he had wanted with the folder. He closed the pages and smiled. "So that, you see, explains the problem."

"No," Longarm admitted, "I don't see."

"Oh." Whitson looked confused for a moment. Then he brightened and tried again. "You see, Vega Zuni is not actually reservation land. Except, of course, for the land covered by the pueblo itself and the fields cultivated under specific Zuni ownership."

"I still don't get your point," Longarm said.

"The Zuni are not the only residents of the, um, valley, Marshal Long. Or Vega, if you prefer. Much of the land is farmed by Mexicans, and there are a number of, um, Anglo families farming there now as well. And of course upstream in the mountains there are the mining interests. Those are Anglo too, of course."

"What does all this have to do with Zuni irrigation rights?" Longarm asked.

"Why . . . everything. It is the mine that has blocked the flow of Rio de las Vegas, Marshal Long. Didn't your department tell you *anything* about the nature of the, um, difficulty?"

"They told me there was a likelihood the Zuni were going to get friendly with the Apache and start a war," Longarm said. His tone was perhaps more testy than he had intended, but he was getting a bit tired of this clerkish popinjay sniping at Billy Vail.

"Oh. That!" Whitson smirked and fluttered his hands some more. "Wild, imaginative rumors," he said, dismissing the whole thing. "The Apache have never been friendly with the Zuni. Besides, the Apache are *quite* settled now, you know. We've established a model farm program and are seeing truly marvelous results. A very civilizing influence, the plow." Whitson smiled. He seemed thoroughly convinced that the Nadene nation was now docile and agrarian.

Longarm would buy that notion along about the time the Nadene menfolk cut their hair short and swapped their horses for oxen. Or commenced beating their rifle barrels into plowshares. So far he hadn't heard of any of that happening.

Still, he kept his silence on the subject. Aside from the fact that no ill-informed Justice Department employee was going to tell this bright BIA man anything, a man tends to learn more when he's listening than when he's talking. And there was obviously a lot here that Longarm did not know.

"So you see, Marshal Long, our problem with the natives at Vega Zuni are a matter of convincing them that they are in the wrong. Nothing more."

Longarm raised an eyebrow at that one.

"You still fail to understand." Whitson sighed. "The mining company is perfectly within their rights, Marshal. They are doing nothing that could be construed illegal in the slightest. They are operating mining claims legally filed on non-reservation federal lands. Just as the Mexican and Anglo farmers have been doing. There is no interference with lands under reservation control. Really we are quite capable of keeping our own house in order, Marshal Long, despite what your department seems to feel. We only asked for your assistance as an accommodation to the Vega Zuni natives. Which, of course, we are most willing to do. We make *every* attempt to cooperate with our wards, no matter that we feel your department's, um, involvement to be unnecessary."

"So I came down here pretty much for nothing," Longarm said.

"In a manner of speaking, I am afraid you did, sir. In another..." He shrugged. "If your presence alleviates some of the concerns expressed by the Vega Zuni families, why, I am sure your visit will be of immeasurable assistance."

"And just what is it you think I oughta do, Mr. Whitson?"

"Why, I should think a visit would be appropriate. You know. Ride down there. Give them a good talking to. They respect you, I understand. They should, um, trust you. Just explain to them that the law permits each group, whether farmer or miner, to live lawfully and peacefully on its own land. And of course that we at the Bureau will act on their behalf toward the, um, protection of their interests. If you will simply explain that to them, why, I am sure that will amply justify the expenditure of your time and effort, Marshal Long."

Longarm stood. "I suppose you could give me directions to this Vega Zuni before I leave?"

"I have a hand-drawn map right here that should suffice." He opened the folder on his desk and found the article he wanted. "And if you wish to borrow a wagon, the Bureau would be pleased to provide one of ours." The big smile flashed again. "It all belongs to the same government, you know, and we each serve the people as best we can, eh?"

"I'm sure we do," Longarm said seriously. "But I think I'd best find my own transportation. I know how busy you gentlemen are on behalf of the Bureau and the government. I don't want to impose."

Whitson accepted that almost as a compliment. It was perfectly obvious that he had no idea he or his agency were being gently twitted. "Anything we can do, Marshal. We will be pleased to cooperate to the fullest."

Longarm thanked the man, shook his limp hand, and got the hell out of there before he ruined the whole thing by breaking up laughing.

Good Lord, but there were times when Custis Long was almighty glad he was not an Indian subject to the merciful protection of the BIA's extra-bright and super-sincere lads.

This here was one of them.

And, come to think of it, Longarm realized as he walked back toward the hotel, he *still* wasn't entirely sure what the problem was down at Vega Zuni.

He expected if he really wanted to find out he was going to have to ask the Zuni themselves, and the hell with starry-eyed and probably self-serving opinions passed along by the BIA. The Nadene a nation of farmers, indeed! Longarm snorted aloud as he mounted the hotel steps.

The funeral seemed to be over. Empty though the streets had been before, now they were busy as men and wagons and horses moved back and forth, most of the traffic concentrating in the neighborhood of Gallup's several saloons.

Although these men and their families had just come from a funeral, their mood was definitely one of celebration. A wake, that barkeep had called it. Hell, Longarm generally saw longer faces than this at Christmastime, including the expressions the kids wore. But then, the children, Longarm realized, would be taking their cues from the grownups about whether they should be happy or sad. It sure looked like this Wilse Howard fella was going to be sorely missed by his friends and neighbors.

25

Longarm checked the time and decided it was still a touch early for dinner. Too early to eat but much too late to look for the liveryman and make a start toward Vega Zuni. He got directions from a smiling townsman just back from the tragedy of the Howard funeral and made his way over to the local sheriff's office, which was located unobtrusively on a side street.

A small, neatly lettered sign over the door read CHARLES DEWAR, SHERIFF, SURVEYOR, NOTARY PUBLIC. Obviously not a man to put all of his eggs into one basket, Longarm reflected. He pushed the door open without knocking and stepped in, pausing just inside the doorway to allow his eyes to adjust to the deep shade indoors.

A rugged-looking gray-haired man with an awe-inspiring sweep of salt-and-pepper moustache was standing behind a broad desk and reaching into a filing cabinet drawer. A considerably smaller man, very well dressed, was occupying the single chair that had been placed before the desk. The older man pulled a mostly full bottle of whiskey from the drawer and placed it down carefully before he looked toward his visitor with a raised eyebrow.

"One of you would be Sheriff Dewar?" Longarm asked.

"That's me," the gray-haired man said. He did not introduce his friend.

"I'm Deputy U.S. Marshal Custis Long," Longarm announced, "out of Denver."

Dewar grunted an acknowledgement that could have been taken for a welcome of sorts. He sat, opened a desk drawer, and pulled out three glasses that looked more or less clean. "Join us for a drink, Marshal?" He uncorked the bottle and poured two drinks, then looked at Longarm for an answer before he poured the third.

"My pleasure," Longarm said.

Dewar tipped the bottle over the third glass and shoved it across the desk to Longarm. There was no available chair so Longarm continued to stand.

"You have business here, Marshal?"

"Not in your jurisdiction exactly, Sheriff, but we like to pay a courtesy call on the local authorities, just to let you know I'll be here and operating in your territory."

"Now that's real nice of you, son. I appreciate it."

Dewar smiled and raised his glass toward Longarm, then drank. "Around here we get so damn many federal scalawags running about that we don't hardly try and keep track of 'em all. I certainly do appreciate your attitude, though. Kinda refreshing for a change."

Longarm tasted the whiskey Dewar had given him. He was not certain what it was—not rye—but it wasn't bad. Dewar's friend had already downed his and was helping himself to a second, pouring for the sheriff while he was at it. The man did not offer Longarm a refill.

Longarm noted that Dewar was being pleasant enough about the intrusion of a federal officer in his jurisdiction. Certainly he was displaying no hostility such as was sometimes encountered with local peace officers. On the other hand, Dewar was not curious enough about Longarm's assignment here to ask what it was.

"I understand you folks've had some excitement around here lately," Longarm said by way of making conversation while he finished his drink.

"The funeral, you mean."

"That's right. Important man, I heard."

"Rich, anyhow," Dewar said.

"Also dead," the unidentified friend put in. He sounded pleased.

"A fella in town told me it was an accidental death," Longarm said.

"So the coroner's jury ruled it," Dewar agreed.

"Convenient," Longarm mused aloud.

"How's that again?"

"I said it was convenient, Howard dying by accident like that and all his records getting mussed up."

"You could say that it was," Dewar said, completely unruffled. He took another drink, and the friend reached to refill both their glasses. "Was it something about Wilse Howard's death that brought you down here, Marshal?"

"No. Never heard of the man when he was alive and sure didn't know he was dead."

Dewar nodded. "As I recall, Marshal, accidental deaths of U.S. citizens, also murders, manslaughter, death by misadventure and such as that, aren't subject to federal statutes. Do I remember my law correctly, Marshal?"

Longarm smiled. He had been put in his place, gently and pleasantly. But put in his place nonetheless. "I believe you do, sheriff." He drained off the last of his whiskey.

"Another?" Dewar offered.

"No, that set me up just right. I thank you for the drink and the hospitality in your jurisdiction."

"Any help you need with anything here, Marshal, official or personal, you feel right free to call on me. Anything I c'n do."

Longarm thanked the sheriff and nodded to the sheriff's friend, then went back out onto the busy streets of Gallup.

A good many of the men he passed on the sidewalks were already well oiled, and it looked like this would be a long and profitable night for the saloonkeepers of the town. The women and children he had seen in wagons returning from the funeral had mostly disappeared by now, and the streets were left to the menfolk and their peculiar form of grieving.

They were a happy bunch, though, and not likely to turn ugly from liquor in this mood of gaiety. Probably their sheriff was right to leave them to the celebrating without interference.

Longarm checked at the livery to make sure he had the directions right—there was no sign of life at the place except the horses placidly chewing hay in their stalls—and went back to the hotel.

Never mind what his watch said. His stomach was telling him he was ready for a meal, then a pull at his traveling bottle of Maryland rye and a good night's sleep before the start tomorrow down to Vega Zuni where he might finally find out just why in hell he was here in Gallup instead of home in Denver.

He yawned a little and had to rouse a waiter out of the hotel kitchen before he could get service there, although the dark-paneled bar attached to the place was doing a heavy business.

Chapter 4

Amazingly, the map Whitson had given Longarm was not only descriptive, it was actually useful. Longarm followed it without trouble after a dawn start and reached the long, green valley of Vega Zuni by late afternoon.

Much of the way he had been traveling through the brown, arid scrub of the broad New Mexico–Arizona desert lands, but for the past several hours the road led upward toward the Zuni Mountains. It occurred to him that the mapmakers hereabouts hadn't been overburdened with inventiveness when they named everything. Down south there were Zuni Pueblo and the Zuni River, and here he was on the flanks of the Zuni Mountains. Damn boring, actually. And now here was Vega Zuni.

Vega Zuni, at least, was a positive delight to the eye once the road topped a final rise and let him look down into the valley.

It was a ripe and inviting swath of intense green amid the sere, brown desert hills behind him.

The vega—park, it would have been called at home— was a patchwork of meadows and fields strung along the banks of a thin stream that would be the Rio de las Vegas, obviously taking its name from the green valley it had carved.

The valley ran for some miles to the east, gently rising and surrounded on both sides by the brown hills. The bottom land, though, was a cool oasis of delightful green, with the fields lying close to the stream and clumps of lovely trees spotted here and there, probably at the whims of the underground water seeps that made the whole thing possible.

It was a lovely and welcome island of color and comfort in the midst of an otherwise harsh and unforgiving land, and it was no wonder it had attracted men who wanted to farm these fields and to raise their families in the shelter of the vega.

Longarm reined in his rented horse and paused on the ridgetop to look the valley over for as far as he could see.

Even from a distance of several miles it was obvious the course of development that had been followed here.

At the low end of the valley, just before the protective hills receded and the land turned into flat, desert-like drabness, there was a small community of adobe houses, each with its adobe fences and adobe beehive oven nearby. That would be a settlement of Mexican families. The adobe houses were grouped below a tall, narrow primary structure that showed a cross and bell tower. The fields in the vicinity of the Mexican community were small and carefully tended. From this distance Longarm could not make out what the smaller crops were, but most of the fields had been planted to corn, tall now and already starting to brown.

Upriver from the Mexican portion of the valley and sandwiched between it and the earliest residents of this particular chunk of land was a second grouping of houses and stores. These structures were built of timbers and milled lumber and obviously were the center of activity for the Anglo newcomers who must have moved onto the empty, arable land between the first and second waves of settlers here.

The oldest settlement by far, and the reason Longarm was here, was the pueblo built on the high ground near the head of the valley.

The pueblo of Zunis who had chosen at some time in the past to move away from the crowded conditions at Zuni Pueblo itself had been built in the old fashion, sat well away from the easy access and possible flooding along the Rio de las Vegas, and perched on a series of ledges on the side of a precipitous bluff on the south side of the river.

From the pueblo the Zuni would be able to see anyone entering the valley miles before anyone could be endangered by attack. The adobe—or more probably adobe-covered stone—walls were built against the natural stone of the hillside like stairsteps and could only be reached by way of ladders from below. The residents could pull the ladders inside with them if they did not feel like company.

Longarm was too far away to see much detail of Vega Zuni, but his knowledge of other pueblos indicated it was unlikely there would be any doors or gates or other form of direct access into the pueblo except those ladders.

The Zuni fields were laid out between the pueblo and the silver sheen of the river, each of them with a uniform amount of water frontage, each family's holdings running long and narrow from the water back toward the pueblo. There seemed to be no fields laid out on the north side of the stream, but there was a wide swath of meadow there, probably communally owned for graze and hay-cutting.

The fields nearer the anglo community, Longarm noticed, were much larger than those at either end of the valley and were laid out in a crazy-quilt pattern, some with direct access to the water but many without. First come first served, he guessed, and devil take the hindmost.

For miles to the north and west Longarm had seen little sign of human habitation. A jacale here and there, a flock of sheep now and then, but no towns or even villages. Yet here, on a small speck of nature's kindness in the midst of so much desert, he could observe three entirely separate cultures with one brief sweep of his eyes from east to west.

Whatever the problem, he realized, it was no wonder the farmers who lived here wanted to stay. Vega Zuni was a beautiful and certainly a peaceful-looking valley.

The road he had followed here forked once it entered the valley, each branch of the track keeping well back from the subirrigated farmlands along the stream—which really was too small to be seriously called a river, no matter what someone had chosen to name it.

The first of the three branches led nearly straight ahead toward the church and the adobe-walled Mexican community. A middle fork made for the Anglo village. The third held on toward the east, toward the head of the valley and the distant pueblo on the other side of the stream.

31

He would need a place to sleep and somewhere to take his meals while he was here, so he chose the middle fork when he kneed the horse into motion again.

The pueblo-dwelling peoples he had encountered before had been uniformly friendly but not exactly hospitable in the way a white man would understand hospitality, and he had heard that the Zuni were the most private of all the pueblo tribes. Mostly for religious reasons, or so he'd been told, practically no one except a member of the community was ever so much as allowed inside the walls of the closed pueblos. It would have been futile, and embarrassing to the Zuni as well, for him to approach the pueblo and expect to stay there.

The middle fork of the road zigged and zagged between unfenced fields of corn, barley, and beans until it reached a wooden bridge that was several times broader than seemed necessary for the slender flow of water it covered.

Actually, Longarm thought, it seemed almost wasteful to bother putting a bridge here at all when a man could ride through the Rio de las Vegas without wetting his boots. But then, he had no idea what the flow was like during the rainy season in the low mountains to the east.

It had been some time since he had passed any live water, and the horse was probably thirsty. He knew that he was. He reined the animal away from the bridge and rode beside it into the dried mud of the streambank and on out to the water.

At least for a part of the year, he could see from the muddy, discolored banks, the Rio de las Vegas almost seemed to live up to its name. The bed was a good thirty feet across and showed recent water marks for nearly all of that width, yet now there was only a shallow flow in the middle that could not have been any wider than eight or nine feet.

Longarm stopped the horse in the creek and loosened the reins so it could drink if it wished. The animal dropped its muzzle to the water and snorted loudly but did not drink.

While he was waiting for the damned creature to make

up its mind, Longarm bent low in his saddle and scooped up a handful of the water for himself.

He sipped the water, then screwed his face into a scowl and spat. Clear and sweet though it looked, the water of the Rio de las Vegas tasted lousy.

A sound of bright laughter came from his left, and he looked toward the bridge he had just avoided. A tangled mop of yellow hair was all he could see there. A rather small tangle of yellow hair, at that.

"Something funny?" Longarm asked with a smile.

There was a sound of giggling, then the hair raised a bit higher to reveal two intensely blue eyes and a dirt-smudged small face.

The child—he could not tell yet if it was a boy or a dirty-faced girl doing all the giggling—inched into view a bit more and laughed again. "I thought you was gonna take a drink. I shoulda told you, mister, but I wanted t' see what kinda face you'd make."

The youngster—a boy, he could finally see—stood up and grinned. The kid looked to be seven or thereabouts. He was wearing a pair of tiny bib overalls but apparently not much else. He had a handful of pebbles. He laughed again, picked a pebble out of his palm, and expertly skipped it across the small creek, getting three hops in the little space that was available to him for that time-honored purpose of small boys everywhere.

"Well, I expect I'd've done the same when I was your age," Longarm said with a smile.

"You ain't mad, mister?"

"Naw."

"All right then." The kid selected another pebble and gave it an underhanded toss, but this time the stone hit the water surface with a splash and sank without skipping.

"I'll tell you what, though," Longarm said, reining the horse toward the bridge that separated them.

"What?"

"I figure you owe me a favor for not warning me about that water."

"Yeah?" The kid frowned and eyed Longarm with skepticism. "What fer favor'd that be?"

"Well, I happen to be looking for a place where I could rent a room. Unless you have a hotel here."

"Naw. No call for hotels aroun' here, mister."

"That's kind of what I expected. But if you could point me to a place where they might have a room to spare, I'd call you and me square and give you a ride behind my saddle while we go find it."

The suspicious look in the blue eyes vanished, and the boy's eyes got wide. "You mean that, mister? You'd let me ride on that ol' pony with you?"

"I believe that's the agreement I offered," Longarm said seriously.

The youngster tossed the rest of his pebbles down and scrambled onto the bridge.

"Do we have a deal?"

"We sure do, mister. We don't have no horse. Just a couple dinky ol' mules, an' I ain't allowed to ride them."

"All right, then."

The kid chuckled and giggled with anticipation while Longarm sidestepped the horse over to the bridge so the boy could slide onto the animal's butt and grab hold of Longarm's coattails. The youngster had that slightly yeasty odor of unwashed small boy that Longarm remembered from a very long time ago.

"All set?"

"Yes, sir." His grip on Longarm's coat tightened.

"Just set easy now and go with the movement of the horse. Set up over him, and you won't fall off."

"Yes, sir." But the grip did not lessen in the slightest.

Longarm kneed the horse forward, and the animal climbed the really not too steep south side of the creek bed to reach level ground again. Longarm could feel the clutch of the youngster's small hands as the horse lurched up over the lip of the streambed.

"You're doing fine," he said.

"This is great, mister."

Longarm smiled. It had been a very long time since he had found the idea of sitting on a horse to be a thrill. But there had been such a time once, and this small boy's pleasure brought it back to his memory.

"You'll have to tell me where to go, you know," he reminded the kid. "And it wouldn't hurt for me to know your name."

"Randolph Alvin Martin, Junior," the boy said proudly. "But mostly everybody calls me Bubba."

"Bubba, huh. That sounds like you must have a sister," Longarm guessed.

"Two of 'em," Bubba admitted with no pride whatsoever. Longarm could guess at the face he would be making.

"Well, you can call me Longarm, Bubba. I'm a deputy United States marshal, but all my friends call me Longarm."

Bubba giggled and held tight onto Longarm's coat.

"You hadn't forgot that you're pointing the way, have you, Bubba?"

"No, sir. I mean Longarm." He got up nerve enough to loosen one small hand and pointed. "That house right over there, Longarm."

"That your place, Bubba?"

"Sure is, Longarm."

"You think your folks will mind you dragging home a stranger, Bubba?"

"Aw, my ma won't mind. I'll tell her. My pa's dead, so I'm the man o' the house now. That's what she says her own self. I'm the man o' the house."

"I'm sure you do a good job of it, Bubba."

"Yeah. But I druther not. I still miss Pa."

"What happened to your dad, Bubba?"

"Damned ol' well caved in on him and Mr. Gus. Ma and Miz Farris got Mr. Gus out in time, but Pa suffercated before they could get him up outa there." He paused for a moment. "'Bout that word I just used, Longarm . . ."

"I won't tell your mother, Bubba."

"Thanks."

"You doing all right back there, Bubba? You think maybe we should lope the rest of the way?"

"Could we?"

That, Longarm figured, would distract Randolph Alvin Martin, Junior, from the unpleasantness of the conversation. He touched his spur tips to the flanks of the horse and took the animal into a slow, rocking lope while Bubba held tight to his coat and squealed with pleasure at the new speed and motion.

Chapter 5

Mrs. Martin seemed too young to have a child Bubba's age, but in addition to the boy there were his two younger sisters, one whose age Longarm guessed to be five or so and the smallest still in diapers. The lady had been caught doing washing, and when Bubba and his new friend showed up at the door she hastily grabbed a small towel and dried her face and hands and then tried to tidy her hair before she greeted Longarm and extended a hand to shake his and welcome him. There was a pretty blush of pink in her thin cheeks, probably put there, Longarm guessed, by a combination of the heat from the boiler on her stove and the embarrassment of having been caught by a stranger in her disheveled condition. She really was quite attractive, though, if very thin.

Longarm guessed that times were tough in the Martin household since the passing of Bubba's father and that the young woman—she could not have been very far into her twenties—was giving the most and the best of what they had to the children.

In a breathless rush of excited words, Bubba did his best to perform the introductions and explain his purpose in bringing Longarm to the door.

"We got room, Mama. He can stay in the loft with me, I never wet the bed any more, an' he let me ride on his horse an' it was fun, an' can't we let 'im stay, Mama, please?"

Longarm smiled at the youngster's intensity and marveled at his ability to get so much out seemingly in a single breath. He looked over Bubba's blond head and winked. "I do need a room, ma'am. And of course I'd be willing to pay. Extra if you could provide board as well as the room."

"Oh my, I hadn't considered . . ."

"I don't want to press you, ma'am. It was just a thought. Be quite a favor to me if you could, but I certainly don't want to put you out."

"It's just that . . ."

"Longarm's a federal U.S. marshal, Mama, an' he's my friend too. 'Sides, I said he could, an' I'm the man of the house now. You told me that, remember?"

"So I did," she said lovingly to the small, serious boy. She looked back up at Longarm, having to tilt her chin high to do so. She was really quite a small woman. "You are a marshal, Mr., uh, Longarm?"

"It's Long, actually, ma'am. Custis Long. Longarm to my friends." He smiled. "Like Bubba. And I'm just a deputy, not the marshal."

"I see." She seemed a bit easier about the idea once she had that information. "You should understand that we haven't a spare room. Just the one bedroom where the girls and I sleep and Bubba's loft."

"Why, Bubba and I get along just fine, don't we, pal?" He reached down and ruffled Bubba's already unruly hair. The little boy grinned like Longarm had just given him that horse he had found so thrilling to ride. "As for the compensation, ma'am . . . ?"

Mrs. Martin frowned in concentration, obviously trying to work out a figure that she thought would be fair but probably having no idea what should be appropriate. Hesitantly she said, "Would two dollars be too much?"

"With the board, ma'am?"

"Oh, yes. Of course. With the board."

"Why, I reckon two dollars a night would be fair," Longarm said. Hell, the government would be paying for it. And not the Justice Department either. With this deal, him coming down here at their request, the costs would be passed through to the Bureau of Indian Affairs. The way Longarm viewed most of them, and Dalton Foster in particular, the money they paid to Mrs. Martin might well be the best public service the BIA performed all this year.

"But I meant . . ." Mrs. Martin sounded startled.

"Two dollars a night isn't enough, ma'am?" Longarm

38

interrupted. He knew damn good and well what she'd meant. He deliberately misunderstood the difference between a daily and a weekly rate.

"No," she said quickly. "Two dollars a night will be just fine." Her hands fluttered nervously and knotted in the towel she was still holding. Longarm could see in her eyes, though, that this was good fortune beyond anything she might have dreamed. Actual cash money was probably a seldom-seen commodity for a young widow this far out from any real town.

He reached into his pocket and counted out a week's room and board in advance and was pleased at the way Mrs. Martin's eyes glistened at the sight of silver and gold coins.

Bubba whooped with joy and insisted on taking Longarm's horse to tend to it, first assuring his new friend that he was an old hand at such, as he always took care of the mules as one of his regular chores.

Longarm smiled as he watched the youngster lead the rented horse away. Then he turned back to Mrs. Martin. "I'll try not to put you out more'n I have to, ma'am."

"You . . . I take it you're here on business, Mr. Long?"

"Yes, ma'am. Something about Zuni irrigation water, though I haven't got a straight answer yet as to just what the problem seems to be."

The brightness in Mrs. Martin's eyes quickly faded, and they were clouded with sorrow.

"Did I say something wrong, ma'am?"

"No, it's just . . ." She straightened her shoulders and set her face into stern impassivity. "This whole damned water problem is what . . . is what led to my Randy's death, you see."

"I'm afraid I don't see, ma'am. Bubba led me to believe he died in an accident. A well cave-in?"

"Oh, I didn't mean directly, of course. He wasn't murdered or anything like that. But no one needed a dug well before . . . you know."

"That's the thing, ma'am. I don't know."

The young widow made a face. "Damned Zums," she said bitterly.

39

"Zums?" It was a word, or an expression, or something, that he was unfamiliar with.

She smiled. "I suppose I'm not really making much sense, am I? Why don't you come inside, Mr. Long? I'll make you some herb tea and explain."

"That sounds nice, ma'am." He suspected that locally gathered herbs were having to substitute here for expensive beverages like coffee or real tea. He removed his hat and followed her inside after she shooed the older girl off to collect eggs and swung the baby onto her hip.

"It seems strange to hear someone calling me 'ma'am,' though, Mr. Long. My name is Jane." She smiled. "Not Mama."

"Yes, ma' . . . Jane. I'll swap you that for Longarm instead of mister."

"All right." She settled the little girl on the floor with a pile of bright-colored pebbles for toys, pushed the wash boiler to the back of the stove, and put a coffee pot in its place.

"You were saying something about Zums, Jane?" he prompted.

"Yes. Them." She made a face again. "It's really the Zuni Mountain Mining Company. We've gotten in the habit of shortening that to Zums."

Longarm grunted. Whitson had said something about mining, although the man hadn't been specific about the mining firm or the problem they represented to the Zunis.

"The Zuni Mountain Mining Company—"

"Zums will do fine, Jane. The whole thing's a mouthful."

"Yes, well, the Zums came in here, oh, some time last year. We hardly paid any attention to them while they were starting their mine up there. They seemed much too far away to worry about, and they are not neighborly. Their men keep very much to themselves up there. No excitement to bring them down here, I suppose."

Longarm pulled out a cheroot, waited for her nod of permission to light it, and settled back to let her tell the story in her own way.

"It was quite a while before we noticed that the mining that finally went into operation was having an effect down

40

here in the valley. The quantity of water flowing in the Vegas diminished. For several weeks it actually stopped altogether. Some of our men rode up to see what the problem was. The Zums had built a dam. They said they needed use of the water to power their steam engines and . . . whatever else it is they do in a mine; I certainly wouldn't know. Anyway, they explained that they would only be detaining the water temporarily and then they would release it downstream as always." She frowned.

"As always, indeed. The water level never has returned to what it used to be. Worse than that, though, the water they do return to the Vegas is tainted. Acids of some sort. Some of our people got together and sent off samples to have them analyzed. The water the Zums are kind enough to let down to us is contaminated with copper sulfates and sulfuric acid and half a dozen other things. I can't remember all of them. But can you imagine? The idea of releasing acids for children to drink? It's horrid, that's what it is. Horrid. So now we can't take our drinking water from the Vegas any more. We had to dig wells. But bad as that is, Longarm, that isn't what worries us so. The copper sulfates, you see, are even worse than the acids. All of us use the river to irrigate our fields. Those crops are our livelihood. And the copper sulfates are ruining the soil. If we can't find some way to make the Zums stop contaminating our water, our fields will be permanently ruined.

"You may have noticed when you rode in how brown the corn crop is already. This early in the season it should still be growing. It should still be green."

He had certainly noticed the color of the cornfields, but he had not been familiar with the growing seasons here and had had no reason to suspect that the condition was unnatural.

"This year's crop will be stunted. We will produce much less than in the past. Next year . . ." She shuddered. "Next year the men say we might not get a crop at all. Unless something can be done to clear the water."

"Surely there must be a law . . ."

"We've tried that, Longarm. We pooled our money and

sent a delegation all the way to Santa Fe. The governor said he couldn't help, so we hired a lawyer. It was awfully expensive. We might've saved our money for all the good he did us. The way the government sees it, everybody is acting legally. Us, the Zums, everybody. We farmers are entitled to raise our crops. The Zums are entitled to mine their claim. Everybody is entitled to do what they are already doing. Everybody should be happy." The young woman looked close to tears now. "Except if we let things go on lawfully, the way they have been, we will all be ruined. This whole valley will be ruined, Longarm. We can't let the Zums do this to us. And we won't."

There was a steely conviction in her voice when she said those last words. And Longarm began to suspect that not only was there a threat of violence in the wind from the Zuni side of the affair, there could also be trouble with the other farmers at Vega Zuni, white and possibly Mexican too. And no wonder, if their homes and their livelihoods were at stake.

Longarm drew on his cheroot and accepted the cup of juniper tea Jane Martin placed before him.

In a corner of the room the smallest Martin child sat gurgling and playing with her bright pebbles, presenting an impression of domestic innocence that was not borne out by the events taking place around her.

Longarm very nearly made the mistake of promising to take care of it.

But, dammit, there just might not be any solution to the problem if that Santa Fe lawyer was right and everyone was acting within the limits of the law. The same law that Custis Long was sworn to uphold.

He grunted softly and took a taste of the herb tea.

Chapter 6

There was no saloon in the Anglo portion of Vega Zuni, nor indeed any stores or public buildings of any sort. The few large structures Longarm had seen from a distance and assumed to be stores turned out to be a grainery, a communal coldhouse—sort of like a root cellar on a larger scale—and an equipment shed that included a smithy owned by no one in particular but available for the use of all, including tools that were certainly owned by someone but which were left at the home-built forge for neighbors to utilize as they wished. It was an odd sort of set-up, Longarm thought, but these folks seemed to find it workable for their needs.

The closest they came to having a saloon was the home of an elderly farmer who had no family but who had the knack of turning bulky corn into easily transported corn whiskey.

Bubba showed him to the house, then scampered for home before he got into trouble for being so close to the forbidden territory.

Longarm did not have to announce himself. A dozen or more men were seated on rickety chairs and wood-chunk stools in the dogtrot connecting the two parts of the shack. All of them had half-pint jars of a clear liquid in their hands. The manufacture of non-taxpaid whiskey, of course, was against federal law, but if no one pointed out where the stuff had come from Longarm did not have to inquire about it.

"That Martin's boy Bubba brought you over here, mister?" someone asked as Longarm approached the place.

43

"That's right." He pulled out a cheroot and lighted it. "Mind if I have a seat?"

"He'p yourself. Drink t' go with that set-down?"

"Now that's mighty nice of you." Longarm kicked a log trunk section near the wall and sat on it, leaning back and crossing his ankles. A wrinkled, sunburned old man, probably the manufacturer of the whiskey, handed over a crockery jug and a jar. Longarm poured for himself and returned the jug.

When he tasted of the stuff he smiled and sighed. "Lordy, I haven't had anything that nice since I left West Virginia."

The old man grinned, exposing toothless gums. "None of them sweetners, y'see. That's the secret. No sugar or lasses, y'see. Double run, sour mash an' all as natcheral an' pure as a good woman's tears."

Longarm nodded and solemnly tasted the whiskey again. It was as light and mellow on the tongue as a wisp of cloud on a summer's morning. "Now that's fine. Who do I owe for it?"

"Nobody," the old distiller said.

"We all pitch together from our corn crop," another man explained. "Belongs to all of us, like. You bein' kin to the Martins, I expect you're entitled to a share."

"I'm not kin to the Martins," Longarm said.

"No? Figured you must be Randy's brother. You do favor him some in looks."

"Not from West Virginny," another man put in. "The brother's from back to Randy's home. Ohio. South part. Not West Virginny."

"But if you ain't kin . . . ?"

Longarm gave the old bootlegger a wink and made a show of thoroughly appreciating another taste of the illegal whiskey before he introduced himself. "The government sent me down to see if I could help with your problems here," he explained.

That was not a lie. So they had. And if he was able to do anything to benefit the Zuni, which was why he was really here, these men and the Mexican farmers downstream would benefit equally. He saw no point in getting any more specific than that.

"Well I'll be go to hell," someone said. "Looks like that trip to Santa Fe done some good after all."

Longarm did not bother to correct that impression. The government, federal or territorial or whatever, might need all the good will it could muster in the days or weeks to come.

"Nobody told us you was coming, but we're almighty glad to see you, Deputy. Almighty glad."

There was a general round of hand-shaking and introductions, the names flying so thick and fast that Longarm could not begin to keep up with them. What he could figure out with no trouble was that these were good, rock-solid citizens. The kind of slow and patient men who could live comfortably at a pace geared to the turning of the seasons. The kind who would be slow to anger but who, once pushed beyond their patience, would have a steady, stolid stubbornness to match the patience that had been exhausted. Longarm wondered if anyone at the Zuni Mountain Mining Company knew what kind of fight they were in for if these quiet men decided they'd had enough.

The men were not at all reluctant to talk about their troubles, and they spent a considerable amount of time explaining to Longarm the difficulties Jane Martin had already tipped him to.

"Yield's bad this year," one man said. "Twelve, fourteen bushel to the acre, I'd say."

"Eleven and a half," another man injected.

"Should be forty bushel."

"I cropped forty-two last year. Near forty-three."

"You're fulla shit, Mel. You got a gnat's ass over forty, same as me."

"Don't matter exactly what the numbers was. A good year, hell, a man can bring in fifty bushel if he works at it. Point is, this year it won't be close to half what it should be."

"An' next year maybe nothin' at all."

A man whose name Longarm thought was Ed reached for the jug and helped himself to a splash of corn. "We

45

only got so much of this stuff put by, too. What are we gonna do if it runs out?" He grinned at old Ice—probably a contraction of Isom, Longarm guessed—who made the whiskey for them all.

"Got to move out surer'n hell if that happens," someone else said. "Man can't get along without his toddy of an evening."

"Or his woman afterward, eh, Bobby?" The man who said that looked too dried out and aged to still be thinking about that on a regular basis, but that seemed to be a false impression. His friends, except for the man named Bobby, laughed. Bobby got red in the face. Longarm suspected that Bobby was not long married, although he was probably in his late thirties. Then it became clear that Bobby was not married at all.

"How 'bout that, Marshal?" someone asked.

"How about what?"

"Ol' Bobby over there, he'll be worrying are you movin' in on the widow Martin. Got an eye for that li'l lady, he has."

"Huh," someone else injected. "Can't say as I blame 'im. If I wasn't married I'd be snortin' after her myself."

"Snort away, Joe. It ain't the bellowing that makes a bull, it's what he's got in his whang."

There was a round of laughter, and this time it was Joe who flushed.

"You know, boys, I think this here marshal they sent us is smarter'n us. You notice how he's settin' there not saying nothing while we carry on. Yessir, I got to feel sorry for ya, Bobby. You got some competition after all."

Bobby looked uncomfortable, so Longarm said, "Now boys, I'm just a passin'-through man and not looking to take what isn't mine."

"Yeah, but a man wouldn't mind the borry of something even if it ain't his'un," one of them laughed.

Bobby, though, snuck a look toward Longarm that was grateful.

"Not to change the subject," Longarm said to change the subject, "but you boys aren't planning anything around here that I wouldn't approve of, are you?"

"Who, us?" The man who said it, Joe, was unable to keep a straight face when the words came out.

"I kinda thought so," Longarm said. "And I do understand what this business means to you. But I'd sure like a chance to look around and come to some conclusions before things get out of hand. You know. To where I can't tend to 'em."

The farmers sobered then. For several long seconds none of them was interested in looking Longarm in the eyes. He waited them out.

Finally old Ice, the bootlegger, spoke for them all. "Nothin's been asked, exackly. Nothin's bein' promised, exackly. But we won't none of us do nothing that'd be awkward for you, sonny. You'll get your chance."

"I couldn't ask fairer than that," Longarm said. He smiled. "But I might ask for a refill." He held his now empty jar out, and Bobby was quick to tip the jug over it for him.

Longarm felt fairly good after that. At least one faction of the valley had been defused, however temporarily.

But he still had to face the Zuni, who were the real and present problem here.

He sat back and enjoyed the excellent corn whiskey Ice produced.

Interesting. Yesterday he had seen but had not paid particular attention to a small but rather revealing fact about the roads in Vega Zuni. There was only the one leading into the valley and the three branches from it to the small villages of Zuni, Anglo, and Mexican farmers.

And no road, not even along the creek, linking those three separate communities.

Apparently the three groups didn't mix together a whole hell of a lot. Each worked its own fields and socialized among its own kind as well. Otherwise there would surely be a road running the length of the valley instead of just the one in and out.

Longarm had no particular desire to ride all the way back out to the turkey-foot intersection just so he could follow the east branch over to the small pueblo where the

47

Zuni faction lived, so he reined the horse off the road at the bridge again and followed the Rio de las Vegas upstream toward the mud-colored walls of the pueblo.

It was early, but already there was plenty of activity in the fields as men and some women too started their backbreaking work for the day. Here in the middle of the Anglo farms there were a few pieces of machinery in evidence as mules or heavy-bodied horses pulled cultivators, but at the extreme eastern and western ends of the vega the work was all being done with hand tools.

As Longarm left the last Anglo field behind and came to the long, narrow, precisely laid out Zuni fields, he could see that virtually all the Zuni planted the same self-sufficiency crops and arranged them in very much the same order: corn closest to the water, then beans, and finally low-growing, leafy squash farthest away from the water source.

He was not sure—everything he had ever learned about farming as a boy he had damn sure tried to forget in the years since—but he thought the Zuni, probably because they were closest to the source of the mining contaminants, were the hardest hit by the sudden change in the water.

Now that he was close to it he could see that their corn was runty and poor. Already browning, the tassels should have been at least reaching to saddle height. Instead the tops of the stalks rose barely higher than his knees, and it was rare to see a stalk that had set more than one sheathed ear of corn.

On an impulse he reined the horse close to a mound—downstream the Anglos planted in rows, but the Zuni stayed with the older practice of planting their maize in three-seed mounds—and bent down to snap a tough, fibrous husk from its scraggly stalk.

When he peeled back the outer layer of husk there was damn little revealed. Little that was useful, that is. The immature cob was only partially filled with hard, tiny kernels. If this sample was representative of what was happening in these fields, not only would the stalks yield few ears but each ear would bear not more than two-thirds the amount of grain it properly should.

Longarm frowned and dropped the poorly filled ear.

For a farming community, yields like that would be a disaster as terrible as fire or locust or tornado.

Perhaps all the worse, because this particular disaster was man-caused.

A farmer learned to accept and live with whatever he was sent by God and nature. But a man he was apt to fight.

Longarm glanced to his right and saw two pairs of dark, solemn eyes peering at him from behind a clump of corn. Two children, dusty and dusky, with crude-handled hoes in their hands and wariness in their eyes. He smiled at them, and they turned to dash out of sight into the field they had been working.

He continued on until he reached the eastern branch of the road. There was no bridge here, only a now shallow ford that had been improved with the addition of flat rock slabs until there was virtually a stone-paved road from bank to bank. Longarm guided the horse onto the road and followed it toward the pueblo.

His presence was certainly well known by now. He had been watched steadily ever since he left the last Anglo farm behind him, and probably for longer than that.

No one moved to greet him, though. Young and old, the men working in the fields stood in silence to watch and perhaps to wonder but never otherwise to so much as acknowledge his passage across their land. When he came near they stopped what they were doing and stood immobile, staring, until he was past them.

It could have been unnerving if he did not have good cause to be here.

No one waved; no one smiled; no one so much as turned his face away from the white intruder.

Longarm stopped beside a man who was chopping weeds away from his beans near the road.

The Zuni paused in his labor, braced the blade of his wide hoe on the ground, and leaned on the handle. His eyes met Longarm's but his expression was set and unreadable.

"I'm looking for your headman," Longarm said.

The Zuni did not so much as blink.

"I am Longarm. Your headman sent for me." It occurred

49

to Longarm that he should have asked Whitson who he was looking for here at Vega Zuni. He had neither a name nor a title, although he doubted that "chief" would be appropriate for a pueblo-dwelling tribe. Headman would probably do, if any of them spoke English. Surely someone here had to. He couldn't see Whitson learning the Zuni tongue or even Spanish.

The Zuni farmer did not respond in any way. After a moment his eyes shifted to the right.

Longarm's head snapped around in that direction, and he had to deliberately stifle an impulse to reach for the double-action Colt that rode at his belly. He was getting jumpy, he realized.

A man was coming toward them, stepping out with long, firm strides and moving with considerable dignity for a man in a hurry.

The Zuni was not tall, but he was heavily muscled and fit. His hair was chopped abruptly short just below his ears and showed hints of gray amid the black, but his face was unlined and his eyes were clear and intelligent. Longarm had no clue as to his age. He could have been anywhere from forty to sixty or more. There simply was no way to tell.

Longarm thanked the farmer who had ignored him and dismounted, waiting for the approaching Zuni to reach him.

The man was taller than Longarm had first thought, the immense width of his chest and shoulders making him seem squat from a distance. He had a homespun shirt and trousers and wore an intricate necklace of beaten silver set with white and red stones of some kind. He had on a floppy-brimmed old Kossuth hat that had been decorated with a band of more silver inlaid with white, red, and black polished stone.

If this wasn't the headman, Longarm decided, he damn well should be.

The Indian stopped in front of Longarm and stood in patient silence, not exactly blocking the way on toward the pueblo but certainly not welcoming the visitor either.

"I am Longarm. Deputy Marshal Custis Long from Denver. I believe you sent for me."

The Zuni did not smile, but at least there was a slight softening of his expression. "Long Arm?"

"Yes." Longarm extended his hand.

He had to wait a moment before the headman decided to accept it.

"I am . . ." He said a name that would have required a double-jointed tongue to duplicate. "You call me Hank." He might actually have said Honk, but Longarm was willing to settle for anything familiar.

"All right, Hank." Longarm pulled out two cheroots and offered one to Hank before he bit of the tip of the other and held a match for both of them.

There was no ceremonial puffing of smoke in the six directions of wind and earth and sky, as there might have been with one of the plains tribes Longarm was more familiar with. The Zuni headman known as Hank simply lit up and smoked the thing the way anybody would.

There was also no thank-you given.

Hank drew on the smoke, his eyes narrowed against the rise of it under his hatbrim, and gave Longarm a close and critical inspection from Stetson to boot toes.

Longarm could not decide if the man was satisfied with what he saw or not, but after seconds that stretched out to seem like minutes, Hank grunted softly and said, "Come."

Without another word, the man turned and began walking back up the road toward the pueblo.

Damn friendly bunch, Longarm thought.

He decided it would not be polite to ride when the headman was walking, so he slipped the reins over the head of his horse and set out on foot behind Hank with the horse trailing.

Yeah. Friendly.

Chapter 7

They walked the length of the fields to an open, plaza-like area at the base of the hill beneath the pueblo but went no farther. The pueblo itself was for those who belonged there and for no others. Hank gave neither apology nor explanation. He simply led the way to a fire circle near an ancient, stone-walled well, and sat, motioning for Longarm to join him.

Out in the fields, Longarm had seen no one but men and boys. Here, near the old well, were mostly women coming down the ladders to the well and a few men, artisans who were busy hammering silver pesos into workable plate and some older women who were shaping moist clay into pottery ready for firing. The younger women and girls carried water in huge pottery ollas, balancing the heavy containers with the ease of lifelong practice even as they moved up and down the stone stairsteps and ladders of the pueblo.

Steps worn by the use of many generations had been cut into the rock of the hillside as far as the base of the pueblo walls. From there the Zuni had to mount crude lodgepole ladders to reach the high, inaccessible doors.

From so far beneath the rooftops Longarm could see little of the pueblo itself, although now and then he could catch a hint of movement above the protruding vigas. With no level ground inside the walls of the pueblo, much of the outdoor life of the residents would take place on the roofs. But most of the daily lives of the Zuni would take place in a privacy no white man was likely to penetrate.

What he could see right now was very likely all he ever would see or know about these people.

Even the simple religious ceremonies of hospitality would not be shared with him by the headman.

A doddering man wearing nothing but a ragged loin-cloth wandered near and stopped to show Hank an exquisite brooch of carved silver inlaid with chips of black stone, said something in his strange tongue, and wandered dreamily away without ever once looking at the stranger who sat beside the headman. The craftsman looked just about as old as the pueblo, Longarm thought.

"Nice work," he said. One of them had to open the conversation, and Hank seemed in no hurry to do so.

The headman grunted. "We trade. Sometimes. Get more silver." He looked at Longarm for the first time since they sat. "Have plenty silver now."

Longarm suspected that was a warning of sorts. A reminder, as if one were needed, that the Zuni could buy what they wished—including guns, if that was what they chose.

The Mexican silver could create beauty. Or death.

Hank looked away from him. "You see our fields."

"Yes. They are poor this year."

"Since the other whites come. Very bad this year. Next year . . . ?" He lifted his shoulders.

"You have talked with Agent Whitson about this," Longarm said.

Hank's response was to turn his head away and spit.

"Yet you wanted me to come," Longarm persisted. "You asked for Long Arm."

"We trade sometimes. We talk. We hear. Some say Long Arm is fair." The headman gave Longarm a long, slow look that he could not decipher. "Others say no white man is good." Again there was that undertone of warning.

These people were teetering on the edge, Longarm realized. They could go either way now.

"The white men are just the same as red men," Longarm said patiently. "Some are good, others are not. I do not believe all Zuni are bad. I do not believe all Zuni are good. It is the same with my people. But I believe we are all people. We live. We work. We die. We all want to do these things in peace."

54

Hank grunted again and stared off into the distance, beyond the hills that rimmed the long valley.

"Our people have been at peace for many years."

Hank raised his arm, pointing from the head of the valley and sweeping his pointing fingers down its length. "From the time of my grandmother's grandmother's grandmother the clans of my people have planted these fields. My..." He used a word Longarm did not understand. "...planted there with a digging stick. I worked this land when I was a boy. Since the time of my grandmother's grandmother's grandmother my people have never been hungry here."

Longarm suspected that that part might have been something of an exaggeration, but the point was certainly taken.

"Your Agent Whitson and his uncle who is called Foster tell us we do no wrong." That reference confused Longarm for a moment until he remembered that to most pueblo peoples, the roles of father and uncle as whites know them are basically reversed. But any reference to Foster still confused him. Foster was not the sort to leave the comforts of the clubs and drawing rooms of civilization. If the man had ever actually come here to meet the Vega Zuni headman, it would be damned well astounding.

"They tell us," Hank was going on, "that the white men who poison our land do nothing wrong." Hank looked into Longarm's eyes again. "Is it then right for my people to be hungry? Is it then right for our crops to wither and our children's bellies to swell with hunger?"

"It is not right for a child to be hungry," Longarm agreed.

Not that it looked like any were. Today. Next year... well, the man had a point. Next year the Zuni children would indeed be hungry if the Rio de las Vegas was poisoned.

The headman nodded. "It is wrong. But Agent Whitson and his uncle say they are right, the men who burrow in the ground like the red ants." Hank looked grim. "I say they are wrong."

It was very much here the way it was downstream with the Anglos, Longarm saw. Everyone could clearly see what was right and what was wrong. The problem of course, was that the law was concerned with the law, not with right and wrong.

"You asked for Long Arm to come," Longarm said slowly, thinking rapidly and taking his time about getting the words out. "I came. My place is very far from here. When I heard that you needed me, I came. I have done what you asked. Now there is something I would ask of you. Give me time to see and to learn. When I have learned we will talk again. Until then, I would ask that your people work the fields of your grandmother's grandmother and hammer the silver into things of beauty, eh?"

"We make things of beauty, yes. But soon it will be time to trade, eh?"

"But not before we talk again, yes?"

The headman looked toward the head of the valley for a long time before he answered. Finally he nodded. "Not before we talk again, Long Arm."

It was what Longarm had hoped for.

Neither man had ever actually mentioned guns or Apaches or anything else that was threatening. But both men knew.

The agreement was tenuous, but it was there. The Zuni would do nothing until Longarm had had his chance.

Beyond that there were no promises.

Longarm rose and extended a hand. Hank shook it. Longarm considered that to be a breakthrough of sorts.

"I will come again. We will talk then."

"Yes." Hank stood and, without a goodbye, turned away toward the silversmiths who were squatting over their work.

At least he hadn't tried to put a time limit on it, Longarm thought. But, looking at the dark, unfriendly faces around him, he realized that the time he would be given was not limitless.

He sure as hell hoped he could come up with an angle —*any* angle—that a smart Santa Fe lawyer hadn't seen.

It was either that, or there would be some hell to pay at Vega Zuni.

He reclaimed his horse and swung into the saddle. It

was time to have a look at this Zuni Mountain Mining Company.

The Zuni Mountain Mining Company's operation was further than Longarm had thought, a good four-hour ride east and up from the Zuni pueblo, most of it up more than east.

There was no road linking the valley and the mine, but there were ancient game trails that showed signs of having been used as footpaths too, probably by generations of hunters coming out of the valley below.

Before he reached the mine headquarters itself he came to the first of a series of small dams built in a stairstep pattern in the stream flow out of the mountains. The dams were fairly crude affairs built of mud packed against a base of saplings, much like clumsy beaver dams. They held water, though, plenty of it. Each holding pond contained a dozen acres or so of slightly greenish, definitely smelly slime tailings from the mine workings.

Longarm paused beside the first of the three dams but did not allow the horse close enough to drink the foul water, and he knew better himself than to taste it now. The wonder was that it cleared enough in its rock-tumbled journey down to Vega Zuni that he ever could have thought it palatable to begin with.

A greenish-yellow scum of bubbly stuff like acid soapsuds rimmed the overflow of the uppermost pond. Each succeeding lower pond was slightly clearer and less offensive-smelling than the one above it.

Above that last pond—or first, coming down from the mine—the Rio de las Vegas was a stinking thing. Its course there was lined with dead brush, not a trace of green leaf showing on any of the gray, dry, woody stalks that remained where willowy growth once had been.

No wonder the farmers were angry, Longarm thought, having to live downstream from something like this.

And if the fouled outflow from the mine would do this so quickly to the growth nearby, it only stood to reason that the same devastation must inevitably occur farther downstream as the poisons accumulated beyond the limited capacity of the holding ponds to filter them out.

He rode on, still climbing slightly, until he came within sight of the Zuni Mountain Mining Company.

Like many of the outfits he was familiar with in the mineral-rich mountains to the north, the Zum headquarters was more small town than commercial operation.

Several tunnel mouths yawned darkly from the mountain sides, easily open to view here so far south where there was no need for snow sheds and changing rooms built over them.

The need for the Zums to use so much water was easily visible too at that first look.

Instead of using carts or conveyors to bring the ore down from the shafts to a reduction or processing mill, the company had chosen to use water instead. The ore was carried in a slurry, essentially a thin, dirt soup of river water and mineralized ore, that flowed from mixing tanks at the tunnels through sluice boxes to reach the mill built on the floor of this high, narrow valley. There the ore would be recaptured from the slurry for processing, and the waste water—the portion of it that had not escaped or been otherwise used—was returned to the original river bed.

It was actually a very efficient system. As long, that is, as the operator did not give a damn about the quality of the water that was returned to the Rio de las Vegas.

From a money-making point of view, it made plenty of sense. From the viewpoint of the farmers downstream . . . well, that was something else again.

Aside from the mill beside the river, there was also a collection of buildings. Several large, hotel-like structures must be the boarding houses for the mine workers. A company store, a company saloon, a heavily shuttered structure that resembled a smaller version of the boarding houses . . . Longarm suspected that one of them would be a company whorehouse. And a set of stone buildings, very handsomely constructed, he guessed would be the company offices and the superintendent's home.

All damned efficient, he thought. Except for that one little problem.

Beyond the town he could see a set of narrow-gauge railroad tracks leading in from somewhere to the east and probably connecting eventually with the transcontinental line that lay to the south and also a pipeline of cypress planks that had been laid from somewhere upstream.

A wry smile tugged at his lips and thinned them.

The Zums were perfectly willing to dump their wastes on the people below them, but thier own water needs were filled by the Rio de las Vegas from someplace well upriver from the fouling of the mines and the mill. This section of the river was so bad now that they had to pipe in clean water for their own use.

He nudged the horse forward.

Chapter 8

"Superintendent Carter?" Longarm leaned forward and extended his hand to the small man with gray, thinning hair and nervousness in his eyes. When Longarm introduced himself, though, Carter gave him a broad smile of genuine welcome.

"It's a rare pleasure for us to see someone from the real world out there, Marshal."

"Longarm. Please," he invited.

"Then you must call me Charles," Carter said pleasantly. The given name fit. Longarm could not imagine this harried-looking and quite proper little man being called Chuck or even Charlie. He was working in coat and tie, no informality even in the privacy of his own very nicely appointed office. He was definitely a Charles.

"One moment, Longarm." Carter raised a finger, left his desk, and went to the door to give an instruction to his secretary. "Would you find Chief Bennett and ask him to join us, please, Robert?"

The secretary nodded and hurried away on the errand.

When Carter returned to his office he went not to the desk but to a handsome sideboard cabinet. The lid lifted to reveal a set of sparkling, crystal stemware and racks of fancy, unlabeled bottles that came into view mechanically with the raising of the walnut lid.

The superintendent selected glasses and a bottle without inquiring about his guest's preferences and poured three glasses of what turned out to be a select and very aged brandy. But still, unfortunately, it was brandy, at least the way Longarm saw it. He accepted the drink as a well-intentioned welcome, though, and kept his mouth shut otherwise.

By the time the brandy had been poured and distributed, the third glass being set near the second of the two chairs that faced Carter's desk, Robert was back with a large, heavily muscled man in tow.

The newcomer was wearing a suit but no tie. His shoulders looked like they would burst through the seams of his coat if he made any sudden moves. That situation was not helped at all by the twin bulges Longarm noticed high on both sides of his massive torso. Shoulder-holster rigs, and filled with something big enough to knock a man down and stomp on him with each and every shot. There was something in the man's eyes that said he would be perfectly willing to do just that, too, if the need—or opportunity—arose.

"Deputy United States Marshal Custis Long, I'd like you to meet Leon Bennett. Chief Bennett is our chief of security." Carter smiled nervously. "And a most excellent head of security, if I may say so."

Bennett looked Longarm over slowly before he gave the briefest ghost of a smile and extended his hand. "Long," he repeated, mouthing the word carefully. "They call you Longarm, I believe. I've heard of you."

"That's right. Longarm. And you, I take it, would be the Lee Bennett they call Buster." It wasn't really a question. Longarm had recognized the man immediately from newspaper pictures he had seen. Many of them. Buster Bennett was a very popular man with certain types of glory-hound news correspondents from the Eastern papers and magazines.

Buster. The name hadn't come to the man back when Bennett was a cute-as-pie little boy. Assuming he ever had been a cut kid like little Bubba Martin back in Vega Zuni. More likely Buster was a bullying son of a bitch when he was little and just never grew out of it.

The nickname Buster came later.

Chief of Security Bennett was indeed a buster. A buster of strikes. A buster of heads. He'd gotten his start in the Montana gold fields, if Longarm remembered his reading correctly, improved on it during the Deadwood rush, then really hit his stride out in California during the last dying gasps of those gold camps, after the big companies moved in and needed a real head-breaker to make damn sure the unions could not get a toehold there and cut into corporate profits with such foolish ideas as decent wages or working conditions.

Buster Bennett's union-busting tactics were consistent: quick, efficient, and bloody. He would find out where organization meetings were to be held and then wade into the middle of them with a hickory axe handle swinging at any and every head in reach. Truly stubborn opponents tended to disappear. Bennett invariably explained that the missing gentlemen had been persuaded to leave. In the middle of the night. Somehow, these men never took time to pack or to say any goodbyes.

Yet the man enjoyed a popularity with the big-business-controlled press that bordered on adulation.

Longarm had never met the man before. The last he'd heard, Bennett was still out in California somewhere. But he had damn sure read a bellyful about him.

His kind, seen by the know-nothing reporters, was touted as a living legend of law enforcement.

Longarm's personal opinion was that Buster Bennett was a living bag of shit that ought to be wrapped tight in some of those same newspapers and thrown out on the nearest dump. He gave law enforcement a bad name.

Some of what Longarm was feeling must have showed in his eyes, because Bennett's face hardened and he began to show a red flush of quick anger above his soiled collar.

Charles Carter missed all of that, continuing to smile and nod and motion for both men to be seated and enjoy their brandy.

After a moment of silent challenge, during which Longarm could feel the hairs at the back of his neck prickle and rise, the two turned away from their very private encounter and took the seats Carter innocently showed them.

"I asked Chief Bennett to join us, Longarm, on the assumption that your visit here is an official one. Naturally, both Chief Bennett and myself will do anything within our power to cooperate with you if one of our people has ... shall we say, run afoul of your professional interests."

"Nothing so drastic as that," Longarm assured him with a smile. Regardless of what he thought about Buster Bennett, Charles Carter seemed a sincere and genuinely likable man. "Far as I know, I haven't any interest in any of your folks here."

"Now I'm very glad to hear that, Longarm. We try to hire only the best here, and we like to treat them well. I shouldn't like to find that our faith in our people has been misplaced, and frankly it would surprise me very much if that were so. But, naturally, our own interests are not above the law. No, indeed, nothing like that. So, anything we can do ..." He smiled and held his palm outward in a show of sincerity. He leaned forward, flipped open the top of a highly polished box, and pushed it toward the two men across the desk from him. "Cigar?"

"Thanks." Longarm selected one of the plump, pale-leafed cigars that probably cost more than a meal in a first-class restaurant and clipped the end of it with a sterling silver nipper that had its own velvet-lined niche in the humidor. Bennett took one too but he used a pocket knife to cut his. When Longarm offered a light from his match, Bennett pretended not to see and struck his own lucifer.

"What I wanted to talk to you about," Longarm said when the cigars were properly drawing, "was the interests of the Zuni Indians who live downstream from your operation. The Zunis are wards of the federal government, you see, and my office represents their interests as part of our duties." The cigar was incredibly mild.

Carter smiled. "I understand the problem completely, Longarm. And believe me, I do sympathize with them. Our attorneys in the territorial capital have been fully briefed on this matter and, I believe, have already responded to inquiries from other affected parties downstream on the Rio de las Vegas."

"Parties which you do *not* represent, seein' as how there's no laws been broken," Bennett put in quickly.

Longarm ignored the intrusion. "I understand ..."

"May I fill you in on a little background, Longarm?"

64

"Please do."

Carter steepled his fingers under his chin and leaned back in his chair. He gazed thoughtfully toward the ceiling for a moment before he spoke.

"The Zuni Mountain Mining Company has invested heavily in this operation. A total capital investment to date in excess of three hundred thousand dollars. That figure does not include long-term haulage and rate commitments to the Gallup and Pacific Rail Road, which is capitalized separately but which, frankly, is owned by many of the same shareholders who make up this corporation. This is truly a tip-top, first-class endeavor, Longarm."

"I could see that much when I rode in," Longarm agreed.

"Of course." Carter smiled again. "Now, mind you, we have absolutely no legal obligations as to the *quality* of the water we discharge. That point was researched most carefully by our legal staff before we commenced engineering design work, I assure you. There are certain requirements as to the *quantity* of water discharge. All of those requirements are now being met or exceeded, Longarm. Actually exceeded." Carter dropped his hands into his lap and leaned forward, closer to Longarm.

"In spite of this, Longarm, the company spent . . . invested, I should say . . . an additional and otherwise quite unnecessary thirty-five thousand dollars, actually a bit more than that figure, in the construction of settling ponds within the river flow downstream from our operation. Three separate ponds, Longarm."

"I rode past them on the way in," he said.

"Good. Excellent. You saw them, then. Yes, over thirty-five thousand dollars, for their construction, and all of that constructed voluntarily and at our expense for the sole purpose of being good neighbors to those downstream from us. Our engineers assure us that the silting effect in those ponds will insure a clean water flow downstream for years and years to come, and—"

"They aren't working," Longarm said.

"I beg your pardon?"

"I said those settling ponds aren't doing the job. I'm

sure your engineers did say that. They were wrong. I've seen the fields down there. Maybe you have too."

"As a matter of fact, Longarm, I haven't had time that I can spare away from the press of my duties here, but—"

"The ponds aren't doing a lick of good, Charles. That's acid that's reaching the fields down in that valley, and if it keeps up there won't be any fields left to plant down there within a year or maybe less."

Carter shook his head. "We are exceeding every requirement, *every* requirement the territorial government has imposed on us, Longarm. At a staggering expense to our shareholders. And with virtually *no* return on the investment capital to date, Longarm. I must say that the shareholders have been generous, actually quite generous, in their willingness to go the extra mile toward neighbor relations. But, as I am sure you can readily see, this is a major undertaking. Truly a monumental effort here. And now our job is to produce a profit from that investment. Surely you can agree that we have already done far more than was required of us. Now we wish only to be left in peace to do our jobs. As we are quite willing to do for our downstream neighbors as well. This . . . harassment . . . by the settlers in that valley, their lawyers, now by the Zuni also . . . we have done absolutely everything that in good conscience we must, Longarm. We have done that and more. Surely you understand that."

The man was sincere. Longarm believed that. Charles Carter was concerned with operating this mine and producing a profit. From the way he kept mentioning capital and shareholders, Longarm suspected the little man was under considerable pressure. But he honestly had no idea what effect the mine wastes were having on the people downstream. He had no idea . . . or wanted none.

"Law's damn clear 'bout it," Bennett said. "You got no beef here, federal man."

Carter brightened and smiled again. "Nor we with you, Longarm. Our intention is to cooperate to the fullest with the law in all its forms, and you are welcome here today and at any time in the future. I shall certainly do everything I can to assist you, and I know Chief Bennett has precisely the same outlook. We are law-abiding businessmen, Longarm." He rose. "And now, sir, may I invite you to be our guest at lunch?"

Longarm sighed and stood. What these people were doing here was criminal. Or at least it should be. The point was, it was indeed within the law. And even though Charles Carter's employers were ruining the lives of dozens of families downriver from here, there just was no way Longarm could dislike Charles Carter personally.

The little man was honestly proud of the efforts the company had made beyond what was lawfully required. And he honestly had no idea of the devastation that was being done anyway.

When Carter led the way toward the door Bennett leaned close and whispered, "When you're done, federal man, you drop over to the honkytonk. I'd like to have a word, just you an' me."

Longarm nodded without looking at the man and followed Carter out of the office.

Chapter 9

Lunch was a pleasant affair in the dining room at the superintendent's home. Although Longarm had not announced himself beforehand and there could have been no way for them to know he was coming, the service was laid out on the long, polished table as if the corporate officers were expected, and Mrs. Carter presided from the foot of the table with gracious formality.

Service was provided by a middle-aged Mexican couple, and Longarm suspected the Carters would have dined in such elegant comfort with or without a guest present to justify the formality.

There was no place for business talk at Amelia Carter's table, and at midday no notion of retiring to the parlor afterward for brandy and cigars. This, after all, was a working day, and Carter seemed anxious to get on with his job. When the meal was done the superintendent gave Longarm a warm but nonetheless brisk goodbye and headed back toward his office at a swift pace.

Longarm pulled out a cheroot and took a moment to light it and look around the company town again before he ambled downhill toward the company saloon.

This was a closed camp, purely a company town, of course, but in many ways it resembled any other small mining camp, complete with livery, store, saloon, and whorehouse. The livery corrals, though, instead of housing draft stock, mostly held a collection of Rocky Mountain canaries, the ubiquitous burros that originally had been used as cheap pack animals by the early prospectors and which now were invaluable for their small size, easy keeping, and ability to work underground without ill effect. The burros, he knew, would be used to haul ore carts along the narrow rails laid inside the tunnels of the Zum mines.

Longarm walked past the closed and shuttered whorehouse, probably open for business only at the shift changes, and by the company store. The saloon was beyond the store, close to the boarding houses for maximum convenience.

He was getting low on cheroots, so he detoured into the store on his way to meet Buster Bennett.

"New man," the store clerk said when Longarm appeared. The man grunted. "Don't look like no mucker, though. Not in them clothes. Don't tell me they brung in another damn engineer."

"No, just a visitor. I need some cheroots. The best you've got."

"You got your pay slip, mister?"

"I already told you, friend, I'm a visitor. I just want some smokes."

"No pay slip, no credit. Them's the rules."

"But I don't want credit," Longarm explained patiently. "I just want to buy some smokes. You know. With cash. You've heard of it, I'm sure." He pulled some coins from his pocket.

"No cash here, mister. Comp'ny credit only."

"Give the man his smokes, Benny." The voice came from the doorway. Bennett stood there, his bulk filling the doorframe and considerably reducing the amount of light that could gain access to the cluttered store counters. "Put 'em on my chit."

The clerk, Benny, blinked once and then hurried to comply with Bennett's orders. The man ignored the boxes of cigars and cheroots on open display and pulled a small wooden chest from under the counter and held it open for Longarm's inspection.

The cheroots were a brand with which Longarm was not familiar, but the long, slender sticks of rolled tobacco looked to be of superior quality, with a pale wrapping leaf every bit as fine as anything found on the most expensive cigars.

"Give the man a fistful, Benny," Bennett said. The big

man slouched against the jamb, and Benny grabbed a handful of the fine cheroots from the box and put them in front of Longarm.

"I'd be glad to pay for these," the tall deputy said.

"On the house," Bennett said.

Longarm hesitated for a moment. Bennett seemed to be wanting something from him. He might well be considering this small favor a bribe of sorts. On the other hand, to refuse such an inconsequential thing as a few smokes would be to cause commotion over nothing. He picked up the cheroots and tucked them into his coat pocket with a nod of thanks to the store clerk.

"You ready for that drink now, Longarm?"

"That I am, Buster."

Bennett led the way back out into the bright sunshine of the afternoon and down the short street to the saloon.

Instead of going to the bar for their drinks, Bennett took a table at a back corner of the sawdust-floored company saloon and turned the chair so that his back was to the wall. Longarm got the impression that this was Bennett's normal duty post.

"Whiskey. Two." Bennett said it without looking in the direction of the bartender, but instantly the man ducked under the bar to find a select bottle, not of counter whiskey but something with a fancy label on it. He brought the bottle and two glasses quickly to Bennett's table.

Buster Bennett ran a very tight ship here, Longarm observed.

Bennett tilted the bottle over their glasses and poured two generous measures. "Long life," he said, raising his glass in a toast.

"Sure." Longarm sipped his drink while Bennett cracked his back in a gulp and poured a refill for himself. The whiskey was a bourbon, probably a good one. It was a shame Longarm didn't care all that much for bourbon.

Bennett sighed loudly and wiped his lips with the back of his hand. "Now that's fitten." He drank the second one slowly and this time waited until Longarm was ready before he poured the refills.

Longarm looked around the saloon. At this time of day

there were very few customers in the place, and those few had the look of confirmed drinkers. Most of the men here would either be underground or asleep, waiting to go underground. After the shift changes would be the busy time here, just as it would be at the whorehouse.

As at the store, no actual money seemed to change hands here. Whenever a drink was delivered, the barman sorted through a sheaf of paper slips and placed the selected chit beside the drink along with a stub of pencil. The man who "bought" the drink would make a mark on his chit with the pencil provided, and that would be that. The cost of the drink—highly inflated, Longarm was sure—would be deducted from his pay.

It was a good system—for the company. A man who enjoyed himself in his off hours could work like a mule for a full tour and end up owing the Zuni Mountain Mining Company for the privilege of having worked for them.

Still, the system was neither illegal nor unusual. It was simply the way things were done. A driller or monkey or mucker who didn't like the system was welcome to work elsewhere.

Longarm set his drink down on the liquor-stained surface of the table and looked at Buster Bennett.

"If I had to guess," he said, "I'd say that you have something more on your mind than being neighborly."

Bennett polished off his third drink, set the glass down carefully, and leaned forward, arms crossed on the table top before him. "You don't like me much, do you, Long?"

"That's neither here nor there, of course, but if it matters, no, I expect I don't."

Surprisingly, Bennett took no offense. In fact, he leaned back in his chair, tipped his head back, and roared with laughter. "By God, Long, an honest fed'ral man at last."

"Now, I'm real glad you see it that way, Buster. Indeed I am. Because you're right. I *am* an honest federal officer. I work at it. I figure to stay that way."

"Good!" Bennett declared. He refilled both their glasses, although Longarm was a long way from needing more. He had barely touched his second drink.

"Let's cut through the bullshit," Longarm suggested.

"You said you wanted a word with me. So let's have it. What's your word, Buster?"

"By God, I think I could like you, Long." Bennett was still chuckling, although Longarm could not see the humor.

"How nice for me," he said dryly.

Bennett waved a hand as if the whole thing was of no consequence. "I just wanted to get t' know you better, Longarm. That's all. Just wanted to get t' know you better." He took a long pull of the bourbon.

"You really expect me to believe that?"

"Matter o' fact, Long, it's the truth. Pretty much." Bennett grinned at him. His face was slack, like a man whose liquor was beginning to get to him. Longarm was not so sure about that. He doubted that a man could gain Buster Bennett's reputation while being a boozer. Unless, of course, he had gained that reputation before the whiskey got to him. Bourbon could be the reason a man like Buster Bennett now found himself way out here.

"Naw," Bennett went on, "I just wanted t' get a better idear of what kinda man you are. Heard some about you, o' course. Heard a *lot* about you, come t' that. But you an' me, we never crossed paths before. Wanted t' know…" He belched loudly and wiped his mouth. "Wanted t' know if we was gonna spit an' snarl or if we could both o' us jus' do our rightful, lawful jobs. You know?"

"Matter of fact," Longarm said, "I don't. What're you getting at, Bennett?"

Bennett helped himself to another drink. Longarm had not yet touched his after the last refill.

"Wanted t' know was you the kind t' get his ass up in th' air, y' see. Wanted t' know if you'd stick t' the law or try an' make your own, y' see." He drained off that drink and poured another. "A man hears things, y' know. Heard you could be a hardass. Sometimes a hardass, he gets t' thinkin' about how he'd *like* things t' be. An' not 'bout the way things *are*. No offense 'ntended, Marshal Long-fuckin'-arm." The big man gave Longarm a loose-lipped grin and took another drink.

"Are you boys doing anything illegal here?" Longarm asked.

73

"Hell no. Which is m' point, y' see. Ever'thin' within th' law. All th' way. But we're shittin' all over them pet Injuns o' yours. Hell, I know that. Ol' Carter, he don't know that. 'S 'truth. He really don't know it. You know it. I know it. But he don't know it." Bennett giggled. The sound was odd coming from such a large man, but he actually giggled. "But it's all inside th' law, lawman. This here comp'ny ain't doing nothing 'cept what's legal. An' tha's my point, y' see." He grinned and helped himself to another drink. He tried to pour more for Longarm, but the glass was already full. He poured anyway, and the bourbon overflowed the glass and ran onto the table. Bennett seemed not to notice.

"You made your point, Buster. And now you know. I swore I'd uphold the law. Nobody ever said I had to agree with it."

"Tha's all I wanted t' know, Longarm. All I ever wanted t' know."

Longarm pushed his chair back from the table. He had had about all he really wanted of Buster Bennett's companionship.

Bennett blinked and leaned forward to clutch Longarm by the wrist. "Jus' so you know," he said. "I don't put up with no shit. Any o' them red Injuns show up here wantin' trouble, me an' my boys'll give 'em a gutful. Them or any other sons o' bitches as wants trouble. We'll give 'em all they want. An' all legal. You keep 'em in line, Long. Or I'll blow their balls off. You 'member that. Pass it along. Law's on *my* side. You 'member that." He laughed and reached for the bottle.

"Yeah. I'll remember that," Longarm said calmly. "Thanks for the drink." He left the table without looking back.

He reclaimed his horse from the hitch rail in front of the company offices and headed back downriver toward the distant settlements of Vega Zuni. At the first holding pond, he stopped and looked back toward the company town for a moment.

Buster Bennett was standing on the porch in front of the saloon staring after him.

Longarm could not tell for sure from this distance, but it sure as hell seemed to him that Bennett was standing square and firm for a drunk. Not swaying a bit.

That was odd, Longarm thought.

And so was the entire conversation he had had with Buster Bennett.

Why would Bennett have wanted to bring any of that up? There seemed no reason for it.

Could Bennett have been trying to decide if Longarm was like himself? The kind of coward who would skirt the edges of the law, hanging there where he could dart out just long enough to do his dirty work and then duck back under the cloak of its protection?

Or was the man just a once-powerful but now pitiful drunk? That was the impression Bennett was giving. Longarm was not so sure he believed it, though. It was an impression too easily gained. Possibly an impression Bennett wanted to give and then belie.

Odd, Longarm thought. And so was that business about Charles Carter. For a man in Carter's employ, Leon Buster Bennett was not exactly respectful.

There obviously were a great many things about the workings of the Zuni Mountain Mining Company that escaped casual observation.

Longarm touched the flanks of the horse to start it down the mountain, then gave the animal its head and let it pick its path while he shifted back in his saddle and leaned against the cantle for balance on this long downhill stretch to the valley below.

He was conscious of the acid stink of the water beside him.

Chapter 10

It was a good three-quarters of an hour past full dark before Longarm finally reached the Martin house on the outskirts of the Anglo community in Vega Zuni. Bubba was outside waiting for him, eager to take the horse and tend to it. And waiting with him was the older girl, whose name was Suzanne.

As soon as Longarm dismounted and Bubba took over the horse's reins, the little girl dashed indoors shouting, "He's here, Mama, he's here, can we eat now?"

Longarm trailed behind her, removing his Stetson and shuffling his feet a bit in unexpected embarrassment. "I hadn't meant to put y'all out, ma'am...Jane...sure didn't expect you to wait supper on me."

"It was no bother," she lied. She had already started feeding the younger girl, who was too young to understand explanations about why she would have been required to remain hungry while they waited for the boarder to appear.

"I never gave that any thought, Jane. I should have. If I'm late again, please don't wait for me."

"If you wish."

"Yes, ma'am."

She gave him a cautionary smile.

"Jane," he corrected.

Suzanne was already waiting impatiently in her chair, and Bubba was quick with his chore of bedding the horse. He was inside and in his place before Longarm had finished washing up.

Jane Martin took an overcooked and somewhat dry roast from the warming oven without apologies and handed

77

Longarm a hefty butcher knife so he could carve the meat while she brought out the rest of the meal.

There was also a pot of steaming coffee, slightly bitter from having been on the stove so long. Longarm gathered that she had been able to replenish her larder somewhere with the board money he'd paid her the day before. He suspected that this meal was something of a treat for the woman and her little family.

Suzanne was about to dig into it but got a softly spoken but nevertheless sharp rebuke from her mother. The children bowed their heads and clasped their hands.

"Would you care to do the honors, Mr. Long?"

There wasn't any graceful way to get out of it. Longarm ducked his head and stumbled his way through a table blessing.

"Thank you."

Nice woman, he thought. Pretty too. But she sure had cooked a dry roast. Longarm smiled and took a second bite. He wouldn't have uttered a word of complaint even if the dry meat choked him. It was, after all, his fault that it was overdone.

"Did you bring us any pretty pebbles, Longarm?" Bubba demanded between gulps. The little boy was getting around all the meat he could handle, just as fast as he could stuff it in.

"Pebbles, Bubba?"

"You know. Like Lindy plays with?"

"And you don't, young man?" his mother teased.

"Aw, Mama. I'm too old for play stuff like that. They're just pretty, that's all."

Jane winked at Longarm.

"No," he told Bubba, "I didn't bring any pebbles. Should I have?"

The boy shrugged. "Sometimes when the men go up to hunt or cut wood or whatever, they think to bring some. All the little kids like them." He put a slight emphasis on "little" there, as if he himself would not be interested. "They're in the river. All up in the mountains there," Bubba explained.

"Well, I'm sorry I didn't know that, Bubba. Next time I'll look for some if I have time to spare."

"Wasn't any time to spare this time," Suzanne said with feeling. "I was *hungry*. I was." She smiled and somehow managed to fit an overfull spoon of beans into her small mouth.

Jane Martin looked embarrassed by her daughter's directness, but Longarm laughed. "My apologies, young lady," he said. "The fault is mine, and I won't let it happen again."

"Good," the little girl said seriously. She took another huge bite.

"You're a fine cook, Jane Martin," Longarm said. "I thank you."

Mrs. Martin dropped her chin and blushed a little.

They walked down to the riverbank. The night air felt good, Longarm thought, just cool enough to be pleasant after the heat of the day but not so cool as to be uncomfortable. Jane had brought a shawl to drape over her shoulders.

"Thank you for helping with the dishes. I don't believe I've ever known a man to do that before."

"Oh, I didn't mind." He smiled. "Kinda thought it would keep Bubba from squirming about it so bad now that he's seen me do it once."

"You know, of course, that you've become his hero."

"I can't say that his judgment's all that good if that's the case, but he's a fine boy. You should be proud of him."

"I am." She stopped at the top of the cutbank near the bridge and looked upriver.

There was a new moon rising, its pale light reflected on the shimmering surface of the water. At night the river was pretty. And any scent of acid it might have carried was being borne away from them by the breeze.

"You like it here, don't you?" Longarm asked.

"More," she said. "I love it. It is . . . my home. The future that . . . that Randy and I had planned here, it is all I have to leave to my children when I am gone."

"I can understand that," he said.

"Yes." She smiled at him. "I thought you would." She

sighed. "You are a good man, Marshal Long. I do believe that."

"Why, thank you, Mrs. Martin." He looked away from her, up the moonlit path on the river.

He felt a trifle awkward, not sure what this slim, attractive woman might welcome, and what she would not. He was finding it difficult, though, to stand so near and see her features in the moonlight and not want to take and hold her.

The children were all abed and sleeping, and the last of the cleaning up had been done. Now...

She turned to face him and moved a step closer. "You are wondering why I asked you to walk out here." It was not really a question.

"Yes."

She moved nearer still, so that the tips of her breasts brushed lightly against the cloth of his shirt. His coat and vest were inside the house. He had removed them when he went to help her with the dishes.

"You are a gentle man, Custis Long. And I, I fear, am a shameless woman. I haven't...I've not lain with anyone since Randolph died. I don't want..." She shuddered lightly, but he did not believe she was cold. "I don't want to accept a loveless marriage for the sake of the farm and the loneliness. Eventually, I suppose. But not yet. Can you understand, Custis Long? Can you forgive me?"

His answer was to take her into his arms.

Her lips rose to meet him, and she was receptive to his touch, her mouth and body hungry as they met his.

He lowered her gently to the grass on the river bank, and her fingers moved eagerly to his buttons.

Longarm shoved his shirttail inside the waistband of his trousers and began to button his fly. At his feet, still sprawled on the grass with a happily wanton smile on her pretty face, Jane Martin was in no hurry to dress. She seemed more interested in watching him.

"Aren't you getting cold?" he asked.

She shook her head, her smile remaining. "As a matter of fact, I feel quite warm and cozy now." She sat up and wrapped her arms around her knees, resting her chin there and looking up at him.

"Okay. If that's what you want to do. But I hear some wagons coming."

With a squeal of surprise, Jane burst into motion then, bounding to her feet and hurriedly pulling her dress over her head.

Longarm laughed and finished dressing himself. There really wasn't all that much need to hurry. The rattle of trace chains and the creak of wooden-spoked wheels was still quite far away.

Jane was dressed within seconds, though, and fussed with the straggling wisps of hair that had escaped from the bun at the back of her neck, as if anyone seeing those must surely and instantly know what she and her house guest had just been doing.

Good thing a glance wasn't as much of a giveaway as most guilty-feeling folks seemed to think, Longarm realized.

He frowned after another moment of listening. "Never mind," he said.

"What?"

"Those wagons. Reckon they aren't on this branch of the road after all. Sounds like they're moving on up toward the pueblo."

"Are you sure? I can't hear them at all."

"Yeah, pretty sure. Several wagons. I can't be sure how many. Three, four, maybe half a dozen. Moving on up the valley now, though. I thought they were heading this way." He grinned at her. "Sorry about the false alarm."

"Beast! You just wanted to scare me."

She allowed herself to be mollified with a kiss and a hug.

He could guess that things in the Martin household were apt to be somewhat changed from now on. He hoped she wouldn't turn out to be a clinger, though. That farmer who had his sights set on the pretty widow—Bobby, was it?— might get some peeved. Longarm could handle that if it happened, of course. What really worried him was that little Bubba might feel hurt by his new friend's sudden

81

interest in his mama. Longarm genuinely liked the kid and didn't want to cause him any hurt.

He wondered if he should mention something about that to Jane, but she brought it up first.

"Could I ask you something, dear?" She moved closer to him and laid her fingertips gently on his wrist.

"Of course."

"I don't want you to misunderstand. Tonight was wonderful for me. I needed . . . not just what you might think . . . but the closeness. Just being held by someone. If you can understand that."

"Yes, I think I can."

She smiled up at him. "Bless you, dear Custis, I believe you just might. But . . . and I don't want to hurt your feelings about this, dear . . . but I don't want you to think you have any claims on me now. Or any obligations to me. Tonight was wonderful. I'm grateful to you for these past few hours. But I don't want . . . well, I don't want to complicate my life, or yours, or the children's. I hope . . ." Her voice trailed off into an awkward silence.

Longarm laughed and hugged her. He felt as if a weight had just been lifted off his shoulders. Hell, she didn't want him clinging to her any more than he wanted her to do it to him. "No need for it ever to be mentioned, ma'am." He deliberately drew out the "ma'am" into a slow drawl. "Nor repeated if you don't wish it."

"Thank you, dear." She came onto her tiptoes to give him a kiss. It was a friendly kiss, not a passionate one, and it was delivered to his cheek instead of his lips.

The ground rules had been established. No one was laying claim to anyone else's time or attentions. That was fine with Longarm. In fact, it couldn't have been better.

They walked together back to the house, comfortable with each other but making no outward display of affection, not even holding hands.

Inside, he told her good night, and Jane slipped quietly into the small bedroom she shared with her daughters. Longarm climbed the ladder into the loft to the bed he would share with Bubba for the remainder of the night.

Chapter 11

"Long! Marshal Long! Get out here quick!" It was the old bootlegger called Ice. He was standing in the Martin doorway, and he looked considerably agitated.

Longarm put down his fork and stood, motioning Bubba to stay where he was. Jane had to take the boy by the arm and forcibly push him back into his chair when he tried to follow despite Longarm's warning.

There was something in Ice's voice that made Longarm suspect this was not a conversation a child should hear.

"What is it?"

"Over here. This way. My God, Marshal, I never seen men shot up so bad. And I thought I'd seen 'bout all there was to see in that line."

Ice took off at a run, and Longarm followed on foot, not wanting to take the time to fit up his horse with saddle and bridle.

"They brung 'em to me, Marshal," Ice said over his shoulder. For such an old fellow he moved right along, and Longarm had to hustle to keep up with him. "Don't know why. Some of 'em come to me sometimes for, uh, somethin' to settle their stomachs. Maybe they think I'm close as this valley's got to a doctor. I don't know. But they brung 'em to me."

Just who "they" were was unclear. Longarm tried to ask, but all he got was a rapid shaking of Ice's head and even greater speed from the old man's legs.

"They" turned out to be several wagon loads of Mexicans wearing the baggy cotton trousers and smocks of peons.

The wagons held picks and shovels and pitchforks. And dead men.

"Jesus," Longarm whispered.

The men who were alive were in a state of tearful agitation, wringing their hands and screaming in Spanish that no one in the Anglo community, including Longarm, seemed able to understand. Longarm could make out some of the language, but certainly not when it was delivered with such fear-impelled speed.

There were, he finally sorted out, five bodies in the several wagons.

The dead men had not merely been shot.

They had been shot to pieces.

Quite literally to pieces. The worst of them was held together at the extremities only by tattered scraps of flesh. The best of them was missing most of his head.

In spite of all Longarm had seen over the years, his stomach turned some flipflops at the grisly remains in the wagon. No wonder the old man had reacted the way he did.

In addition to the dead men, there were three wounded men. The Anglo farmers of Vega Zuni were gathered around them, washing their wounds with Ice's multipurpose alcohol and tying probably useless bindings around the ugly, bloody bullet wounds. Everyone seemed to be trying to ignore the bodies in the wagons, and there were no women in evidence.

At least one of the wounded men was going to die, Longarm saw at once. The peon had been shot very low in the belly and now, after being bumped and jostled for miles in the back of a farm wagon, every breath tore a scream of agony from his pale, dry lips.

That one wouldn't last long. For the peon's sake, Longarm hoped he died quickly.

Of the other two, one would probably lose an arm before his ordeal was over—one way or the other—and the other one had a good chance of recovery.

Longarm looked into the wagons again, at the digging tools there and at the bodies.

It took no great powers of deduction to realize what the peons had been up to.

They too were threatened by the acids in the water they depended upon for their livelihoods.

But their response had been to blame not the acids but the dams that contained the holding ponds.

They had gone up there during the night with the intention of destroying the holding pond dams. It had to have been these wagons Longarm heard when he and Jane Martin were preparing to return to the house.

Longarm shuddered.

Buster Bennett and those "boys" he spoke of had done this. They killed five men—six, maybe seven, once the final count was in—and wounded more.

And these poor sons of bitches had walked right into it.

Worse, they had done it all for nothing.

Even if they *had* been able to break the holding pond dams and let the water down, it would only have made things worse. It only stood to reason that those engineers Charles Carter told him about were telling the truth, just like Carter, as far as they knew it.

Those holding ponds were intended to capture the fouled water long enough for the acids and other crap to settle out. Just because the ponds didn't do the whole job they were supposed to do did not mean that they weren't doing *any* of it.

Without the ponds to slow the contaminated outflow from the Zum operation, the acids in the Rio de las Vegas would be *worse*.

The peons would only have increased the problem if they had been successful last night.

And for that, five or more of them died.

Longarm swallowed back a taste of bile at the back of his throat. Standing there looking at the mutilated bodies in those wagons, he could not help remembering that he had not yet taken the time to visit at the Mexican community downriver. He had talked with the Anglos and the Zunis and even the Zums. But not yet with the Mexicans.

If only he had . . .

85

To hell with that. Worrying about all the things a man had *not* done was a sure road to madness.

He was doing what he could, little though that seemed to be. If he was going to start blaming himself for the faults and frailties of others he might just as well pitch the whole thing and turn in his badge right now. He had faults and frailties enough of his own without taking on those claimed by these poor, sad sons of bitches. The peons had made two bad mistakes, one of judgment and the other of action, and a bunch of them had paid for it with their lives. It was sad, but it wasn't Longarm's fault.

It was, however, his business.

He steeled himself and moved past the wagons again to take another and this time more critical look at the wounds the dead men had suffered.

The men had not merely been killed. They had deliberately been torn apart by bullets beyond counting.

Buster and his "boys" hadn't been content with killing. They had fired time after time, cartridge after cartridge, into men who were already dead.

It had been brutal.

He took another look, first into the wagon beds and wagon boxes, then at the peons who were still alive and unharmed.

As far as Longarm could see, there wasn't a firearm among them, nor anything closer to a weapon than a pitchfork. Here in this flatcrop country the Mexicans were not even carrying machetes.

The peons had been virtually unarmed when they attacked the dams with their shovels and picks.

Their deaths had been as good as murder.

Longarm beckoned for Bobby to join him. The men were all gathered close around the wounded. Bobby was standing at the back of the crowd. He turned away from the others and came over to Longarm's side, carefully avoiding looking into the back of the wagon Longarm was standing near.

"Any of these fellows speak English?" he asked.

"Damned if I know, Longarm. We don't neighbor much with the greasers. Onliest one I ever remember talking to is

86

over there in the back of that wagon." He motioned but did not look.

"Help me see if we can find one that does, will you? I need to get some information here."

"Sure, I c'n do that."

They separated, and both Longarm and Bobby began approaching the peon farmers one by one—there were at least a dozen of them—taking them by the arms and speaking to them.

Either the men had no English or they were too shaken to be able to use it. Longarm received only wide-eyed stares of terror in response to his gentle questions. One of the men looked at him and began to cry.

Then, inexplicably, the group of nervous peons scattered, all of them turning almost in a single motion and racing away into the fields, leaving their dead and their wounded behind as they dashed off with loud cries of fear and warning.

Longarm looked back the way the men had been staring as they fled.

Eight riders were approaching along the river bank, eight men carrying Winchester carbines in their hands.

Eight men with Buster Bennett at the head of the heavily armed troop.

No wonder the peons ran like hell.

Longarm's fingers moved involuntarily to touch the butt of his Colt, to assure himself that the revolver was there if he needed it.

Not that he could do all that much against eight men, if it came to that. And as far as he knew, his was the only firearm in the crowd except for the guns Bennett and company were carrying.

Longarm motioned for the farmers to stay behind him, close to the wounded Mexicans on the ground, and stood with his legs braced and shoulders square while he waited for Bennett to come near.

"Good work, Longarm," Bennett said when he got close enough to speak without shouting. He had left the rest of his men a hundred yards or so back, within rifle range but well outside the accurate range of a handgun, and came on alone. "I see you caught the bastards." Bennett smiled with grim satisfaction. "Yep, mighty good work." He brought his horse to a stop directly in front of Longarm and peered past him to the wagons, the farmers, and the wounded men.

"What the hell are you talking about, Bennett? And why'd you and your people chase these poor souls after what you already done to them?"

"Chase?" Bennett's eyes widened with a shocked innocence that Longarm wouldn't have believed if the President of the United States *and* Billy Vail gave him a direct order to do so.

Whatever Leon Buster Bennett was up to here, Longarm didn't believe it, Bennett knew Longarm didn't believe it, and he was going to rub Longarm's nose in it. The intention was blatantly clear.

"Why, Longarm," Bennett went on, still with that feigned innocence, "I never chased them fellas here. Wasn't even sure who it was we got into a fight with last night, protectin' private property like we were. No indeed, what I come here t' do, Longarm, is report to you that a crime was committed. Of course I know that criminal trespass and assault and things like that ain't exactly in your jurisdiction, I know that just about as good as you do, but I figured, being as you're the closest law we got around here right now, that it was my proper and bounden duty to report it to you first chance I got." Bennett smiled with all the warm sincerity of a coyote charming a chicken. "Sure got to say that you worked fast, my friend, catchin' these felons so quick."

Longarm glared up at the mounted bully. So that was the way it would play, eh?

Bennett's story was going to be that the Zuni Mountain Mining Company holding ponds were attacked in the night by an unknown force of men, and the company's security patrol properly and appropriately fought to drive them off the private property.

Never mind that five men had not only been slaughtered, they had also been stood over and shot to ragdolls afterward. Chance gunshots, Bennett could claim.

Never mind that the peons were armed only with shovels and other tools for digging. It was dark, Bennett could claim.

There had been an attack on private property. That property had been defended.

It was all within the law, of course. Within *territorial* law.

Bennett's snide little jibe about jurisdiction. Shit, Bennett knew that murder by itself was no federal offense. Knew, too, damn him, that no Zuni had been killed last night to bring this incident under Longarm's control.

The only dead and wounded were Mexican peons who would fall under the benevolent protection of the territorial government. Or not.

Longarm felt like puking. Preferably down Buster Bennett's crisp, fresh collar.

The man looked smug as hell sitting high on his horse while a few feet away a gut-shot peon was dying.

"That's the way it happened, huh, Buster? Your boys fought off an attack in the night?"

"Yeah, Longarm, that's just exactly the way it happened." Bennett grinned and reached inside his coat for a cigar. Longarm guessed what he was doing and made damn sure he didn't give Bennett the satisfaction of moving a hand closer to the butt of his colt. Bennett looked almost disappointed. "Lucky for the company we spotted 'em in time to prevent damage to them dams. Woulda been bad if them dams got busted. Not our fault, o' course, but we do try an' be good neighbors." Bennett got such a charge out of that lie that he laughed out loud at the thought of it.

"You're a real son of a bitch, aren't you, Buster?" Longarm said evenly.

Bennett got a charge out of that too. He practically fell off his horse, he laughed so hard.

"I am. I am fer a fact, Longarm," he chuckled when he could get breath enough to speak again. "But within the law, friend. Entirely within the law, y'know."

"Yes," Longarm said dryly. "Within the law."

"Oh, I always operate within the law." He laughed again. "Just like you, my friend."

89

"Was that all you wanted here, Buster? To inform me of the alleged attack on the company's private property last night?"

"That's right. That's all we come down here for." Bennett grinned wickedly. "O' course."

"But it isn't my jurisdiction, just like you said. I expect you ought to inform the local law about it."

"If you say so. I'll get a wire off to Gallup first thing when I get back." He grinned again. "I expect we'll be wanting the sherf to come down here an' investigate. Naturally we'll want to file charges against whoever attacked us. If they can be identified, that is."

He shoved the end of the cigar between his teeth and nudged his horse forward, edging it around Longarm but crowding close. He stared down into the nearest wagon box.

"My oh my," he said. "Now what happened to these fellas? Big fight down in Mextown last night or something?"

"You know. . . ." Longarm started hotly. Then he bit the rest of it back. Bennett was deliberately baiting him, trying to goad him into making assumptions.

Once he did that, Longarm would be leaving himself wide open for Bennett to plant another barb.

Once Longarm identified these wounded or dying men as part of the attacking force, Bennett could thank him and claim that it had been too dark for him or any of his men to identify anyone from the night before.

The slimy son of a bitch.

Bennett grinned at him around the end of the stogie in his teeth. "You were gonna say something, pal?"

"No," Longarm snapped.

"Yeah, well, I done my duty here. I reported it to you. On your advice, Mister Deputy Marshal, me and my boys'll ride back to headquarters and get a wire off t' Gallup. It'll all be up to the sherf then. We already done our duty in the matter."

"Yes. Yes, you certainly did your duty," Longarm said.

Bennett grinned again and touched the brim of his hat in

a mocking salute. Then he wheeled his horse with a flourish and loped off to join his men.

The bunch stayed there at the river bank for a few moments while Bennett spoke to them. Several threw their heads back in laughter loud enough to reach all the way across to the watching, unbelieving farmers who had forgotten for a moment the wounded peons in their care.

"Jesus," somebody breathed.

"Yeah," Longarm agreed bitterly.

Bennett's armed force of hardcases turned around and rode up the valley.

And there was nothing, absolutely nothing, Deputy Marshal Custis Long could do about it legally.

Chapter 12

Longarm did what he could to help the wounded, but that was very little. The gut-shot man took long hours to die a screaming, ugly death, and there was very little anyone could do to help him.

The rule, of course, was that you never give liquids to a man with a belly wound. Longarm overrode that reluctance on the part of the farmers and gave the poor peon all he would take from one of Ice's whiskey jugs, but even the potent liquor was unable to keep the pain at bay. It was a merciful blessing when the man finally died.

The other Mexicans had returned after Bennett and his men were out of sight. No one had suggested that they try to move their injured while the one man lay dying, but now the rest gathered around and began to shift the remaining two wounded and the dead man toward the bloody wagon boxes. Someone—Longarm hadn't noticed who or when in the intensity of his effort trying to ease the dying man earlier—had unhitched the peons' teams and led them off to feed and water. Now the Anglo farmer called Joe motioned for several small boys, Bubba among them, to bring the mules in.

"Wait," Longarm said.

He had no trouble getting their attention. The grim-faced and shaken farmers, both white and brown, were looking to him for leadership.

"Do you speak English?" he asked the nearest Mexican. The man obviously knew enough to understand the question, but he shook his head solemnly.

"I need someone who *hablas* English," Longarm said. "And Bobby, I'd like you to go up to the pueblo and ask the headman to come down here. I have to talk to everybody in the valley. I have to make sure that everyone here understands what went wrong last night. And what would have made it even worse if that *hadn't* gone wrong. Would you do that, please?"

Bobby nodded. Unlike a cowboy or a stockman, who would not have considered making the trip up the valley to the Zuni fields without a horse, Bobby set out afoot, jogging swiftly for a hundred yards or so, then dropping back to a fast walk for forty or fifty yards, then resuming the jog so as to cover the ground quickly but without tiring overmuch.

The Mexicans talked rapidly among themselves. Longarm was able to catch only a word here or there. Finally one of them too left the group and trotted away, moving down the valley toward the Mexican community. Apparently he had gone to fetch back someone who could translate.

Longarm brought out a cheroot to smoke while they waited for the others to gather. He accepted a pull from the jug Ice offered him.

"Bad doin's," the old man said.

"Yes."

"You gonna arrest them yahoos?"

Longarm sighed. "No," he admitted.

"You ain't scared of them. I seen that in your eyes when you faced that man. You was ready to take 'im."

The other men, including most of the Mexicans, were gathering around the two.

"The problem is," Longarm said slowly, "Bennett and his men aren't the ones who broke the law. Our friends here did that. If I had to arrest anybody it would have to be these men here." He motioned toward the peons. Some of them definitely understood some English, because they began to look alarmed. "An' I don't want to do that."

He left the group and walked down toward the murky waters of the Rio de las Vegas. There was no moonlit beauty to be seen in the stream now. It looked foul. It looked much the way Longarm felt.

He stood there, waiting and smoking, until he saw the

Zuni headman Hank coming down the riverbed with Bobby. Off in the other direction a high-wheeled carretta was approaching from the Mexican end of the valley, pulled by a pair of burros like those used in the mines.

Then Longarm went back to the wagons and motioned for the men to gather around him.

When everyone was there, he climbed onto the box of the nearest wagon, ignoring the bodies at his feet. The dead men were beginning to bloat and would have to be buried before nightfall.

"Listen up," he said. "We got to have a talk."

He did his best to explain the situation. Not the law, but the real situation. Mostly the fact that the valley would be in even more danger from the contaminated water if those dams were destroyed.

"Those dams, bad as they are, are the only thing allowing you to make any kind of crop this year. They let some of the acid drop out of your water and go into the ground. Without those dams, your fields will die. Not next year or the year after, but right now."

He spoke slowly, giving time for the Mexican youngster who had been brought in the cart to translate for the others, and giving time too for Hank to comprehend the language that was not his own. From the Zuni headman's intense expression and frequent head shifts, Longarm guessed that the Zuni understood Spanish far better than he did English, for the headman listened both to Longarm and the young translator.

"I can't make you any promises," Longarm said repeatedly, "but I guarantee that your troubles will just get worse if you destroy those dams or if you try to make another raid on the mines. You have to give me time. Please. Give me some time to work on this."

"Our people are dead," the Mexican boy announced, repeating what one of the older men was telling him. "Are we to permit the murderers to be unpunished?"

"It wasn't murder," Longarm explained again. "Not in the eyes of the law, it wasn't. The law says that your men were wrong. The law. . ."

"Fock the law," one of the peons said without waiting for the translator.

Longarm looked the indignant Mexican in the eyes. "Take your choice, señor. If you want justice, I'll try and help you. If all you want is revenge, you're on your own. And I'll arrest you for that just as quick as Buster Bennett will shoot you for it."

The man was still angry, but he turned his eyes away from Longarm's.

Longarm looked at the Zuni headman. "What about your people, Hank?"

"Long Arm has heard my word. No thing has changed."

"Good. Anybody else?" Longarm asked.

There was no response.

"Then leave the damned Zums alone. Leave the mines alone. An' for Pete's sake, leave those dams alone. Give me time to work on this. All right?"

There was no agreement, exactly. But there was no open disagreement either.

"What're you gonna do, Longarm?" one of the white farmers asked.

Longarm climbed down from the wagon box and turned toward the Martin house.

He did not answer.

The truth was that he just plain didn't damn well *know* what he could do to help.

So far, all he came up with was a depressingly long list of things he *couldn't* do.

The law that he had always held in such high esteem had him damned well hamstrung on this one, and there seemed no way he could meet it and justice too.

Bubba slipped inside the shed as Longarm was saddling up. The boy stood against the side wall of the open-fronted structure, his eyes solemn with new-found worry. Longarm knew what the child's problem was. Today he had seen a man die. Today he had seen the badly mutilated bodies of other men. After today, little Bubba would never again be quite so innocent as he was when he woke this morning.

96

His wide, serious eyes kept going from the use-polished grips of Longarm's Colt to Longarm's face and back again.

"What is it, Bubba? Are you wondering if I'll be brought back here in a wagon looking like those Mexican neighbors of yours? Or if I'll be going out now to do the same to someone else?"

He shook his head and refused to meet Longarm's eyes.

"You took a big an' unpleasant step toward growing up today, Bubba. You've seen what men can do to other men." He snapped his cinch strap tight, tucked the loose end into the D-ring of the McClellan, and pulled the stirrup off the seat of the saddle, letting it down carefully so it did not fall free and slap the horse.

"Your mama would've wanted to spare you seeing and knowing such for some more years, Bubba, and I can't say as I blame her. But it's something you had to learn sometime. It's the way things are." He slipped the halter off the horse's head and let it drop against the wall of the tie-stall, replacing it with his bridle.

Then he turned and palmed his Colt, holding it so the boy could see. Bubba flinched away from the dark, blued steel sight.

"Something you got to remember, son. This gun or any other, it's a tool. See that hay fork over there? It's a tool. Long handle. Sharp points. A man uses a tool like that to feed his livestock so that his stock can help to feed his family. Or he can use that fork to hurt somebody with. Same thing with this gun. A man can use it to feed his family. Or to protect the folks he loves. Or to keep the law. But however a man chooses to use either one o' these tools, boy, for good or for bad, you ought to remember that it's the man who chooses. The fork and the gun are both just tools. It's the man using them and the use they're put to that's good or bad, not the tools themselves."

Bubba nodded, his eyes still wide. He said nothing.

Longarm picked up his Winchester, propped against the wall of the shed, and slid it into the scabbard slung from his saddle. He led the horse out into the late afternoon sunshine. "Tell your mama I won't be back for supper."

The boy silently nodded again.

Longarm swung into the saddle and shifted his weight a bit, waiting to see if the horse, inactive the whole day while he tried to help the dying Mexican, was going to throw a fit. The animal was restive but not mean. He let off the bit and squeezed with his knees, and the horse took up a jog toward the river.

Longarm did not turn around to wave goodbye to the boy who watched him out of sight.

There were still lights burning in the Zuni Mountain Mining Company offices, so Longarm stopped there first. It was the supper hour or past, and it occurred to him that he had not gotten around to eating today since his disrupted breakfast. But that could wait. It was an office, not a home, so he opened the door and went in without knocking.

"No," the secretary, Robert, told him. "The superintendent has gone home for the evening. You can find him there if you need."

"I need," Longarm said. He turned, but Robert stopped him before he could reach the door.

"Just a moment, Marshal. You are Marshal Long, right?"

"That's right."

"I believe I heard Harry—he's our telegrapher—I believe I heard him mention that a wire came for you this afternoon, and he didn't know what to do with it. Wait here a moment, would you?"

"Of course."

Robert left his desk and hurried up a set of stairs toward the second floor of the office building. While he was away, Longarm stood and idly examined a drawing hung on the wall. The drawing looked more like a rendering done by an architect than an engineer's dry and stodgy plan. Whatever it was, it showed a most attractive and modern complex of buildings, mills, and tunnel mouths, really more of a town than a mine.

Some of the buildings Longarm recognized. Those had already been constructed. There were a great many more

98

that seemed to be in the planning stage for future development here. The way the planners envisioned it, this Zum headquarters was to become a small city with stores and services and even a beauty of sorts. In the drawing there appeared to be no acids in the blue stream of the Rio de las Vegas, and the hillsides were forested with stately timber, the houses surrounded by flowering shrubs.

The reality Longarm had seen outside these walls was somewhat less lovely.

Robert was smiling when he came back downstairs. He handed Longarm a sheet of flimsy message paper much like the railroads used for train orders. "I was right," he explained.

Longarm thanked him and unfolded the slip.

CANNOT LEAVE GALLUP STOP MURDER
HERE REQUIRES IMMEDIATE SLASH FULLEST
ATTENTION STOP REQUEST YOUR HELP
SLASH COOPERATION STOP SIGNED DEWAR

So Bennett had gotten a wire off to Sheriff Dewar in Gallup. Longarm had wondered about that. Not that the wire would have been particularly alarming, of course. But it was interesting to learn that Bennett had sent it.

Covering his ass, Longarm guessed. Making damn sure there was nothing Longarm or the law could come down on him about for murdering those poor damned peons last night.

Buster Bennett was one shrewd son of a bitch. Longarm had to give him credit for that much anyway.

"Thanks," he told Robert again.

He folded the message form carefully and then folded it over again. Instead of jamming it into a pocket as he might normally have done, he pulled out his wallet and tucked the slip into the leather pocket behind his badge.

The message from County Sheriff Dewar was, in effect, a request from local authority for federal assistance.

If any question of jurisdiction ever arose, Longarm

could use that bit of paper to greatly expand the scope of his authority.

A grim smile thinned Longarm's lips as he left the Zum offices and walked down toward the superintendent's quarters.

Chapter 13

By the time Longarm's visit had been announced and he was settled in the parlor with a silver service of coffee and a plate of pastries, waiting for Charles Carter to join him, Buster Bennett was knocking on the door. Either Robert or the telegrapher over at the company headquarters was efficient. Bennett came into the parlor with a smile, a greeting, and no surprise whatsoever at seeing Longarm there.

Not only did he know Longarm was at Carter's home, it quickly became obvious that he also knew about the message that had been delivered. He had probably known the contents of it hours before Longarm knew there was a message for him.

"I'm mighty glad," Bennett said, "that you'll be doin' the investigation o' the attack on our property last night." He gave Longarm a crocodile smile. "A man of your reputation an' everything."

"Yes," Longarm said neutrally.

There would be no investigation, of course. There would have been no point to it. Instead he would get around to dropping Dewar a note explaining the circumstances of the raid and the bare facts of the deaths, and that would be that. The law could do nothing here to further justice. This son of a bitch Bennett knew that, and it pleased him.

Longarm sipped at the coffee and munched at the pastries in silence until Carter joined them. Bennett seemed very much at ease with Longarm's silence. He had the upper hand here, and he knew that too.

"Charles," Longarm said when Carter finally appeared. "I'm sorry to interrupt your evening."

Carter waved the apology aside. "My pleasure, I assure you, Marshal, however unexpected."

"It's about that raid on our dams last night," Bennett injected.

"Oh? Most unfortunate, of course. But Leon tells me his people were able to turn the raiders away successfully. There may have been some injuries, I fear. Leon says an inspection of the scene after daylight showed some blood on the ground. Most unfortunate."

Longarm looked at Bennett, who seemed entirely composed in spite of his lie.

"Six men died, Charles. Six men. Another may not make it."

Carter's eyes widened with horror. "No!" He looked at Bennett.

The big man shrugged. "Longarm is investigating it for the sheriff. He should know. Naturally, me an' my boys didn't know we shot so true. It was dark, y' see. The rest of 'em carried off their dead."

Longarm's jaw firmed, but there was little he could say to explain the truth to Carter. By now the mutilated bodies of the peons had been buried.

"Actually, though," he went on, "that wasn't what I wanted to talk to you about, Charles."

"No?"

"Actually, I was hoping you could take a ride with me tomorrow. Go downstream with me and see for yourself what damage is being done by your operation. I've been hoping that between us we could work out an... accommodation. Something that will keep everybody happy."

"I don't ride, Marshal, and I am told a carriage could not negotiate the grades downstream. That is why I haven't driven down there before now."

"The Mexicans who tried to bust your dams made it up in heavy farm wagons last night, Charles. I don't say it was necessarily easy, but they made it."

Carter smiled. "Then of course I should be glad to accompany you tomorrow, Marshal. As I told you before, I am quite willing to cooperate in any way we reasonably can." He turned to Bennett. "You can handle things in my absence, Leon. I have confidence in that." To Longarm he added, "Leon holds the title of assistant superintendent in addition to his many other duties for us."

This time Bennett scowled. Longarm suspected the big man would much prefer to go along on this ride, to make sure he was able to know if not entirely to control the conversations that might take place. But he said nothing. After all, he could hardly refuse.

"That will be just fine, Charles," Longarm said. "About dawn?"

The smile on Carter's face faded. "Couldn't we make it a more civilized hour than that? Eight o'clock, say?"

"I'll be here at eight."

"I shall leave instructions for a carriage and driver by that time then, Marshal."

"I'll take care o' that myself," Bennett volunteered.

"Thank you, Leon,"

They made some small talk after that, but Longarm was quite frankly in a hurry to get away from Charles Carter's parlor. No matter how genuine the welcome there, small pastries were no substitute for an overdue meal. As soon as he decently could he made he made his excuses and left.

"I'll come with you," Bennett said. "You'll want a bed for the night an' . . . uh . . . whatever else y' need. I'll take care of you, never fear."

"Thank you, Leon," Carter said. Longarm was rather less pleased about that prospect.

On the other hand, someone would have to authorize his food and quarters here, since everything seemed to operate on chits and credit rather than cash.

It looked like he was going to have to put up with Buster Bennett's company for another evening.

But tomorrow, by damn, tomorrow might be different. He was putting a lot of hope into Charles Carter's humanity and sense of fair play. He hoped that confidence was not misplaced.

"Good night, Charles. My apologies to you and your lady."

Carter smiled. "Eight o'clock tomorrow, Marshal."

* * *

"Easier going now," Longarm said encouragingly. Carter looked tired and nervous and out of sorts, but Longarm was not sure if that was because of the trip or because of what they were seeing as they finally reached the floor of the valley with Vega Zuni strung out before them.

They had started out almost on time, with Longarm riding and leading the way. Before they had even gotten below the third dam, though, it was apparent that Charles Carter was not used to driving. Longarm tied his horse to the back of Carter's light, high-wheeled carriage and took over the lines himself.

When he came by the dams the evening before on the way up to see the mine superintendent it was already dark. Now, in daylight, he had been able to see the damage done by the raiding party of shovel-bearing peons.

Damage indeed. The poor bastards with their pitiful tools had hardly scratched the face of the lowest holding pond dam. It was difficult to see where they had tried to breach the thing. Much easier to tell where the five had died.

There was blood aplenty there, and piles of bright-gleaming brass, expended cartridge casings where Bennett and his killers took their time firing into the dying and the dead and then stood within a matter of yards to reload and empty their guns into the bodies again. It must have been a hellofa fun night, Longarm thought bitterly.

Carter, accustomed to ledgers and plans but not to blood, had been a bit queasy looking, although to give the man credit he managed to retain his breakfast. It was after that that Longarm took over the driving.

Now, though, they were at the foot of the last chute carrying the murky waters of the Rio de las Vegas down from the mountains and into the checkerboard fields of the valley below.

The carriage slipped and slid some getting down, but the pull back up would not be so difficult. Coming down, the dragged vehicle was trying to slew out of line behind the matched pair of cobs pulling it. Going up again, gravity would help keep it in place.

104

"Know anything about agriculture, Charles?"

"Enough." Carter looked grim. He hadn't spoken much since they came in sight of the fields.

They rolled over the gravel of the river bed, through the area that should have been covered with clear, flowing water but was not, until they were alongside the Zuni fields.

Zuni men carrying hoes and digging sticks looked at them darkly and silently as they passed, the Zunis who had been working near the river withdrawing slowly before the carriage reached them.

Ahead Longarm could see several Zuni boys listen to their elders, then turn and lope off toward the pueblo. The boys were not hiding, but they were hurrying. Probably going to tell the headman about the strange presence of a carriage down from the mountains..

"Stop here, would you please, Longarm?"

Longarm brought the team to a halt.

Carter climbed down from the padded, sprung seat, paused for a moment to stretch, and then walked over to the edge of the stream.

He palmed water from the Rio and raised it to his face. Longarm thought for a moment the man was going to drink, thought about warning him against that, then decided to keep his mouth shut. Letting Carter find out what it was like down here was the reason for his trip.

Instead of drinking, though, Carter smelled the water first. Then, cautiously, he wet his tongue and tasted it. With a shake of his head he spilled the acid-fouled stuff out of his palm and wiped his hand on the seat of his trousers.

"Well?" Longarm asked.

Carter did not answer immediately. He walked behind the carriage and climbed the low bank to the level of the fields. He went to the nearest corn mound and felt the dry, brittle stalk, then an ear husk. Four plants had come up in the mound, but among the runty, stunted stalks there were only three husks set. Carter snapped one off with a practiced twist of his wrist that hinted he might once have been a farmboy himself and peeled back the husk and thatch of brown silk.

The ear was much like the one Longarm had examined earlier. It too was stunted, and there were only a very few kernels of grain clustered near the base of the cob. The tip was completely free of useful corn.

Carter looked at Longarm and sighed.

"You honestly didn't know, did you?" Longarm said.

"No," the superintendent said unhappily. "I honestly did not know."

"And now?"

Carter sighed again, louder this time. "I . . . want some time to think about this."

"All right. There's a house down in the middle part of the valley where I think we can get some lunch."

Carter nodded. He dropped the uselessly immature ear of corn into the dirt and returned to the carriage.

"We'll talk when you're ready," Longarm said. He took up contact with the driving lines and eased the team into motion. Off to the south the Zuni headman Hank was coming down the path from the pueblo, but Longarm pretended not to see. No one shouted for him to wait, and he drove on west toward the Anglo community and the Martin house.

"Thank you for coming," Longarm said. He made it a point to see that Hank and the man named Obregon Mendez, representing the Zuni and Mexican communities, had places as good as those of the whites who had answered the summons that Bubba and some of his pals had spread among the farmers.

"This is Charles Carter. Mr. Carter is superintendent at the Zuni Mountain Mining Company operations. He has something to say to you, though I don't exactly know what yet. I expect we'll all hear it together."

Longarm sat down again, giving a nervous glance through the door. He had been a little unsure about how the Mexicans would react to Carter now after six of them dying, but Mendez had come to the meeting alone, probably chosen because he had some English. The peon did not look much like a leader of men. But then, their leaders were probably dead and buried by now.

106

Carter stood and shuffled his feet a bit, at first reluctant to meet the accusing eyes of the farmers.

"I have seen what is happening to your fields," he said finally. "I have thought about this . . . at length. It was not . . . it was not our intention to harm anyone. I want you to know that."

There was a murmur of disbelief from the white farmers, but Longarm could read nothing from the impassive expression of the Zuni headman nor from the frowning concentration of Mendez.

"Please," Carter said. "I assure you, whether you believe me or not, it was not our plan to harm you. Only to open and to operate a successful mine."

This time the men were quiet, but Longarm could tell that they remained damned well skeptical. He couldn't blame them.

"As I have already explained to the marshal here, we hired engineers to design holding ponds at our expense. And we constructed those ponds, also at our expense, in an effort to prevent the very problems that you are having now. The engineers told us that the ponds would eliminate contaminants and insure against damage to those of you downstream."

The faces of the listeners, white and red and brown alike, remained cold to this man who represented the Zums.

"Our engineers were wrong, yes, but our intentions were good," Carter said, his voice firm now, explaining without pleading.

"Our intentions toward our neighbors *remain* good. We want, intend, to continue our mining upstream from you. But we have no desire to do so to your detriment. We do not wish to make our profits by destroying your homes," he said passionately.

"You gonna blow those fuckin' dams then?" someone asked.

"No!" Carter said quickly, his eyes snapping toward the man who had spoken. "Good Lord, man, that would be the worst possible thing for us to do. Or for anyone. I am truly, deeply sorrowful for the loss of the . . . gentlemen who

107

tried to take matters into their own hands the other night."
This he said in the direction of Mendez, but the Mexican
did not react. Mendez looked like he had enough on his
plate just trying to keep up with the words that were being
spoken. "But thank God they were stopped," Carter said.
"If anything were to happen to those dams, the water here
would be worse, not better. I understand that Marshal Long
had already explained that to everyone."

Carter paused and challenged them with his eyes. No
one seemed willing to take it up.

"That would be the worst possible thing," Carter insisted. "What are needed are *more* dams and holding
ponds, not fewer. More ponds, you see, so that they will
properly accomplish the job our engineers erroneously
thought the original three would do. More ponds so the
. . . uh . . . effluents, the discharge from our mining process
will be cleared, and it will be clean, usable water that will
be released downstream to your fields. Don't you see? We
did not come here to be your enemies. We came here to
conduct a business. We still wish to do that. But . . . we
hope we can work this out so that both you and we can
prosper, even thrive, as good neighbors sharing the same
streamflow of the Rio de las Vegas."

Carter had their attention now. Even Mendez looked interested, and the stony-faced Zuni leaned back and folded
his arms. Longarm was not sure, but he thought he could
detect a hint of relief or perhaps approval in Hank's dark
eyes.

"What I shall propose . . . and, mind you, I cannot make
any promises until I have discussed my suggestions with
the owners of the company . . . but what I shall propose to
our investors is that we design and construct a more exten-
sive series of step-dams below the existing holding ponds.
The expense of that, of course, would not be small. I cannot guarantee to you that our investors will be willing to
accept the loss of profit until the cost of more dams has
been met. Frankly, gentlemen, we are only now reaching a
point where we can expect some return from the considerable investment required to open the operation. And naturally I cannot promise what someone else will do. But I

assure you, gentlemen, that I will plead your case with my board of directors. I will ask that they authorize expenditures to design and build more holding structures in an attempt to deliver clean water to this lovely valley."

Carter paused, and there was a round of whispers among the farmers. Longarm could see animation, even eagerness, in their expressions for the first time.

"Yes?" Carter was pointing toward a man at the back wall. The farmer stood, and Longarm could see it was Bobby.

"You don't sound like the sonuvabitch we would've expected," Bobby conceded. There was some low snickering of agreement among the rest of the men. "I' give some credit where it's due, Mr. Carter, there's nothin' you say here that gets my back up." More approving murmurs ran through the crowd.

"Well, Mr. Carter, you say you can't make no promises for your bigwigs, an' I reckon I can't make no promises for my neighbors neither. But if it makes any difference, Mr. Carter, you can tell that board o' muckymucks that me an' my mules would be willin' to pitch in an' help you build your new dams. I don't ask no man t' do for me. I ain't afraid of work. I just don't wanta be put off my own land. An' I reckon I'd be willin' to pitch in with the labor if you folks tell me what t' do."

Carter smiled. Bobby's offer was quickly followed by a chorus of similar pledges from the other farmers in the room.

Longarm could feel the tension evaporate from the crowded room. This seemed like a completely different crowd from the one that had filed in earlier.

The farmers practically fought to be the next in line to announce their pledges of labor and livestock to use in the construction of the additional holding ponds.

"Thank you. Thank you, everyone," Carter said eagerly. "I count on your support with this project, and I assure you I will make much of it when I present my plan to the board. Why, your assistance, gentlemen, would keep the costs to the company minimal. Minimal, I assure you. Engineering, of course. Perhaps some equipment repairs, although we have more than enough scrapers and sledges on hand to do the job. A little portland cement." The superintendent smiled hugely. "Why, I am truly encouraged, gentlemen. Truly encouraged. I can present this suggestion to my board at very little cost and as being of immeasurable benefit to you *and* to us. The good will of our neighbors is *important* to ours or to any other venture, gentlemen, and I shall be happy to encourage it. Happy indeed." He grinned. "I daresay I should be *proud* to do so."

Incredibly, this group of men, who had looked ready to spit on Charles Carter when they first came into the meeting, stood now and gave the man a cheer. Carter beamed.

Hell, Longarm didn't feel so bad about it himself.

There were the six dead men to keep in mind. But it was too late to help them now. There was for all practical purposes no way in the world that Longarm or anyone else could ever exact justice on behalf of those six dead peons.

And this plan of Carter's, if he could pull it off with his board—and Longarm couldn't see any reason why he shouldn't be able to do that, given that the farmers were damn sure willing to put in the labor that would have been the big expense to the Zums—why, it could help the whole damn valley, keep the Zunis safe, and likely keep the young Zuni hotheads from touching off another damn Apache war as well.

There just wasn't any fault with the deal that Longarm could see.

He leaned back and pulled out a cheroot.

Mission as good as accomplished, the way he figured it.

He crossed his legs and lit his smoke and let Charles Carter bask in the enthusiasm of the farmers. The little fellow had come here a pariah and was going out a savior. No wonder he was grinning so. He was entitled to feel good about it. So, for that matter, did Longarm.

Chapter 14

They came outside still in the euphoric mood of good will and neighborliness, the farmers crowding around Carter and actually joking with the mine superintendent now. Longarm heard one of the men promise Carter a mess of greens from his garden soon as they came fresh, and several of them were calling their new friend Charlie. Carter endured it all without complaint.

Eventually Longarm tugged him away from the farmers and herded him toward the carriage. They would have to start back soon. Already it was late enough that it would be dark before they got back up to the mining company headquarters.

"The news must be spreading," Longarm said, nodding in the direction of the bridge. A vehicle, a shiny, varnished ambulance with the sidecurtains rolled up, was trotting toward the bridge, drawn by a matched pair of handsome grays that showed some sweat.

Longarm amended his original notion. The ambulance and grays hadn't come from the Mexican community. He was fairly sure of that.

Then he became completely sure after the vehicle, converted to coach use with seats down both sides of the canvas-enclosed box, rumbled across the wooden bridge and came near enough that Longarm could see the two men in it.

Agent Whitson was driving, and BIA District Superintendent Dalton Foster was riding beside him.

"Not bad timing," Longarm said. "What with such good news to report."

Carter took a look toward the coach and frowned. "If

you don't mind," he said, "I prefer to get on the road now." He smiled. "Such as it is."

"Don't you want me to drive you back?"

"No need for that. I could hardly lose my way from here. There won't be any necessity for it. There is one of those gentlemen I am not particularly fond of. Or vice versa, actually. You will excuse me?"

"Sure, but I'd be glad to drive you back."

"No need for that, Longarm." Carter smiled. "I need to spend time alone anyway. Preparing my arguments for the board and all that."

Longarm offered his hand gladly to Carter. "You've done a good thing here, Charles. I'm glad to've met you and proud to know you, sir."

"The thanks are mine, Longarm. Between us I should say that we have done a fine day's work indeed."

Carter climbed onto the seat of his carriage and wheeled it away from the approach of the BIA vehicle. He seemed in such a hurry to avoid the BIA agents that he forgot about Longarm's horse tied at the back of the carriage, and Longarm had to jump to untie the horse's reins. Bubba appeared at his side almost immediately to take the reins from him and lead the animal off toward the Martins' shed.

Longarm stood where he was, watching Carter disappear in one direction while Whitson and Foster approached from the other.

"Gentlemen," he said as they came to a stop.

"Marshal," Whitson said.

"You son of a bitch," Foster growled.

Longarm laughed. "Somebody put a burr under your blanket, Dalton? Remind me to thank whoever it was." He pulled out a cheroot, bit the end off, and spat it into the dust at his feet.

"How dare you run off like that!" Foster demanded. "I gave specific orders that you were to report to me before you did anything. You are operating under my command here, Long. Mine. Not that mollycoddling Vail's now, mister, and I want to tell you—"

"Oh, pull the cob outa your ass an' crawl down here, Dalton, before you puff up and bust or something." He

112

winked at Whitson, who was a typical BIA man, but no worse than most. "We got this whole deal cleared up and everybody happy. Zuni, farmers, miners, everybody. C'mon down and I'll tell you all about it."

If anything, Dalton Foster got even redder in the face than he had been. Longarm wouldn't have thought that possible, but Foster managed it somehow.

"You son of a bitch," he repeated. Whitson hopped down from the ambulance, and Foster reluctantly followed.

"Y' know," Longarm said evenly, speaking around the cheroot that was clamped between his teeth, "you keep talking to me like that, Dalton, and I'm apt to get purely pissed." He grinned. "I don't know as you really want me to do that."

Foster blinked. His face darkened in color and his neck swelled until Longarm thought he might pop his collar button, but this time he did not repeat his opinion of Deputy Marshal Custis Long. He didn't have to. Longarm didn't have a whole lot of doubts on that subject.

What the hell, Longarm thought. He might as well push the asshole just a touch further. "I'm flattered," he said. "You got off your dead ass long enough to ride all the way down here just to help me with this job. That's real decent of you, Dalton."

Longarm was grinning, but there was ice in his eyes. He shifted forward just a bit, and his hands curled into rock-like fists. If Foster so much as whispered just one more word . . .

Foster saw. He shut his yap and turned away, feigning a need to cough so he no longer had to look into those cold eyes and had an excuse to bite the words off before they were spoken.

Whitson looked confused and worried, but he was quick to jump into the breach with a diplomatic smile. "You said you have good news for us, Marshal?"

"That's right. Damn good." Longarm puffed on his cheroot again and waited for Foster to bluster, but the man was careful not to meet Longarm's eyes again.

Longarm explained it to them, smiling and feeling damned good about it despite Foster's presence here.

Naturally Foster would be heading back to Denver with the credit for this solution in his own hip pocket. But the hell with that. The people who counted—the folks who lived in this valley—knew that the gratitude belonged to Charles Carter. And Billy Vail would know that too, just as soon as Longarm returned to Denver himself. As for what the fools in Washington thought, Bureau of Indian Affairs or Department of Interior or Congress or any-damn-body else, well, Longarm really did not care.

Foster could mutter and cuss all he wanted. Billy Vail wasn't going to crawl a deputy's frame over that kind of fool nattering.

Dalton Foster was a fool, but he was harmless.

Whitson, at least, seemed pleased. Relieved, too. "I know I discounted those stories about the Apaches becoming friendly with the Zunis, Long, but quite frankly there have been more rumors flying since I talked with you. Our agent at the San Carlos Reservation sent a wire just yesterday saying he has heard talk about a group of young men planning a breakout of some kind. Talk that they would be heading in this direction. And some contacts at Zuni Pueblo have hinted as much too, although they haven't been willing to actually say anything. But..." Whitson spread his hands.

Foster gave his local agent a look as though he wanted to punch the man. He did not look particularly pleased about what Longarm and Charles Carter had accomplished here.

Ruffled feathers, obviously. The idiot wanted to make sure he could take all the credit. Now Whitson at least would realize that Dalton Foster hadn't even put in an appearance before the situation was resolved.

"Keep an ear open, of course," Longarm said calmly, "but I doubt there'll be any trouble now."

"You've already notified the Zuni here?" Whitson asked. Foster still seemed unwilling to participate in any part of this.

Longarm nodded. "The headman was there at the meeting when Carter made his announcement. He's already headed back to the pueblo, an' you can be sure every Zuni over there will know about it quick as he gets back."

Finally Foster perked up a bit and seemed willing to show some satisfaction.

"Well, that is that," Foster said briskly. "We can go back to Gallup now, Whitson."

Whitson blinked. "Just turn around, sir? I mean . . ."

"Come now, Whitson. There are no facilities here. You told me so yourself. No need for us to spend the night like savages. We can drive straight back."

"But, sir, I . . ."

"Now, man," Foster snapped. "Or have you forgotten who *you* work for, too?" He gave Longarm a glare, but did not feel brave enough to add any expletives this time.

"No, sir," Whitson said glumly. He turned back toward the ambulance. Poor Whitson didn't have a Billy Vail to protect him from the wrath of fools like Foster.

"Nice t' see you, Dalton," Longarm said. "Come again some time." He flipped the butt of his cheroot onto the ground, barely missing Foster's shoe with it. Foster pretended not to have seen.

Longarm watched the two BIA men climb wearily back into their vehicle and turn the grays back toward the bridge.

Strange son of a bitch, Longarm thought.

Then he turned away and began walking toward the Martin house. He was wondering if Jane would be wanting to take another walk by the river tonight after the children were asleep.

She did.

Longarm lay awake, his hands laced behind his head, and a pleasant lassitude lying heavy in his groin after the exertions of last night. Beside him on the lumpy bed little Bubba was sleeping, his fist and thumb tucked close to his cheek in a habit left over from the days before he was the man of the family.

There was not yet any daylight seeping through the cracks near the eaves, but already he could hear Jane stirring downstairs. He heard the soft pad of bare feet, a dull

115

rattle of wood on wood as she pulled stovelengths out of the woodbox and then the sharper, harder rattle of the iron stove latch. She was building the fire. Soon there would be coffee and eggs and fried cornmeal mush. His mouth watered at the thought of it, but he was not tempted to get up yet and go down to join her.

Right now he was feeling no sense of urgency about anything, very much at peace with the world. Particularly with Jane Martin. Last night before he came up the ladder to join Jane's oldest in the loft, she had given him a shy kiss. Shy in spite of the pleasures they had just shared in the moonlight. The kiss had had a flavor of goodbye about it. She had said as much, smiling gently up into his eyes and then with a sigh whispering that she hoped Bobby could learn to be as gentle as this tall, lean man who had reawakened her to living. There hadn't been a whole lot Longarm could have said to that. He settled for kissing her goodnight—and goodbye—and mounting the spindly ladder to the loft.

Now he was not entirely sure how he should act toward her. As a guest in her home, he suspected. That might be for the best. She had expressed no regrets. He certainly had none.

Bubba snuffled and rolled over in his sleep, wriggling deeper under the covers but not really waking.

Longarm thought about a smoke. Not here, though. Another few minutes and the pressure in his bladder would make it necessary to get up anyway. But not quite yet. This lying abed was nice. A man could get used to it.

It occurred to him that he had not yet had a chance to think about it, what with the congratulations and bantering and drinking of the farmers yesterday evening and then the riverside walk with Jane later, but there was something Charles Carter had said when he hurried away yesterday afternoon. Something about the BIA men. He didn't get along with one of them.

Whitson, Longarm decided. Foster certainly wasn't the type to get out and around on behalf of the "savages" he was charged with protecting. So it had to be Whitson, the local agent for the Zuni.

Funny that Whitson hadn't mentioned making a trip to the Zum mines. He hadn't really said all that much about the situation here. Like he wasn't too well informed about it himself.

And Carter had said outright that he had never been down to Vega Zuni, so he and the agent couldn't have met here any time.

Not that it mattered, of course.

What did matter was that now Longarm had to, absolutely had to, get up and head for the backhouse. Last night's used liquor was wanting its way out.

He eased into a sitting position so he would not disturb the sleeping child, stood, and dressed. He did not want to wake Bubba by stamping into his boots, so he carried them downstairs before he put them on.

"Good morning, Marshal," Jane said. Her voice was pleasant but no more than that, establishing the ground rules from here on out, particularly since she wasn't calling him by his nickname now.

"Good morning." He gave her a whispered greeting and tiptoed outside. The little girls were still sleeping too. He noticed that Jane already had the coffee pot on the stove, and she was busy slicing cold mush ready for frying and had a pile of yesterday's gather of eggs ready to cook.

Nice woman, Jane Martin, he thought.

By the time he was done at the outhouse the false dawn was a rosy pink in the east. Another little while and the sun would break over the Zuni Mountains.

There was smoke rising from every chimney Longarm could see, and already a few of the earliest rising farmers were hitched and moving out into their fields.

This was a solid, peaceful way of life, Longarm thought. Not for him. But peaceful. He was only glad that it could stay that way now. It was good to know that in this isolated enclave way the hell and gone in the nowhere country of New Mexico Territory there was a place where three cultures of men with their different colors of skin could work their fields side by side without fussing.

That was something that would be nice to remember in the time ahead when he would have to be dealing with other men who were not so peaceful.

He stood in the cool dawn air enjoying the sights and the sounds and the scent of the valley for a moment, taking it in as a thing he could remember when the memory of it was needed to ease his hopes, and then reached for a cheroot. He probably had time to smoke one before Jane called him in to breakfast.

The slow-paced sounds around him were altered with the intrusion of running footsteps, and a moment later a small, dark-haired Zuni boy no bigger than Bubba came into view.

The youngster was gasping for breath and was bent over and holding his side. He'd been running for some distance, Longarm thought, and had a stitch in his ribs.

The kid spotted Longarm and changed direction to head straight for him.

Interesting, Longarm had time to think, how the Zuni boy knew exactly where to come.

The boy came to a panting halt in front of Longarm and said something that the white man could not begin to comprehend. He gasped some more, drawing air deep into aching lungs, and tried again, this time in a rudimentary Spanish that Longarm was able to follow.

"Come. Fast come."

Something was wrong at the Zuni pueblo, obviously.

Longarm rejected the idea of setting out afoot, the way the boy arrived. Instead he spun and headed for the shed, motioning for the lad to follow. Even allowing time to saddle, the horse would get him there quicker than his boots could.

He saddled quickly, mounted, and pulled the Zuni youngster up onto the horse in front of him.

"Show me," he said in Spanish.

The boy pointed up the valley toward the pueblo, and Longarm booted the horse into motion.

118

His Winchester was still inside the house, but he had the Colt belted at his waist.

From the way this boy was acting, there might not be time to waste getting the rifle.

Chapter 15

There was a group of Zuni men, including the headman Hank, gathered around the well on the flat land beneath the pueblo. There were, Longarm noticed, no women anywhere in sight.

In the midst of the Zuni he could see two horses. That fact had no significance for him until he got close and recognized the team. They were the horses that had been pulling Charles Carter's carriage yesterday.

Longarm felt a cold emptiness in his gut when he saw the pair and realized the implication of their presence here.

Hank motioned with his hand, and the Zuni stood aside, allowing Longarm closer. The boy who had guided him slipped down from the saddle and disappeared into the crowd.

Now Longarm could see that the cobs still wore their harness and were dragging trace chains behind them, still attached to shattered remnants of what had been a doubletree. The carriage, of course, was missing.

"Carter?" Longarm asked.

Hank shook his head. "We have not seen the Mister Superintendent Carter."

"Oh boy." Longarm rubbed the back of his neck. "Where'd you find the horses?"

"Here. At the well. They are thirsty. Could not drink from the river."

"Oh boy."

Yesterday it had all seemed over. Done with. Everyone satisfied. Everyone working together.

Now...

"Have you sent men to look for Carter?"

"No. No men. Our young men, they want to go. I tol' them no. Better they stay. You look."

Longarm understood. If something had happened to Carter, something, say, other than an accident, it was better if the Indians were not involved in it. A dead Zuni would mean war sure as shit, regardless of what else happened. The problem with the Zuni and their Apache neighbors were just barely defused. That fuse could be lighted again by a single exploding cartridge.

"Thanks, Hank. You did exactly the right thing."

"My people are peaceful, Long Arm. A man of peace, this is not the same as a man who is a coward. If you want..."

"You did right, Hank. What I want is for your folks to stay in the fields today. I'll do what has to be done now."

The headman nodded.

Longarm looked around. Past the horses, close to the well, he could see several Zuni who looked to be in their late teens or early twenties. The young men were leaning on tools. The thing was, those tools were Springfield rifles. At first glance Longarm had thought they were hoes or digging sticks the men were holding. Instead, they were quite a different kind of tool.

None of the young men was brandishing the arms. They made no threats. But this was the first time Longarm had seen this particular kind of tool in the hands of the Zuni. It worried him.

"Keep your people here," he repeated.

Hank nodded. "For now, Long Arm."

"For now. That's all I ask."

He turned the horse away.

It would take him twenty, thirty minutes or maybe more to go back to the Martin house and fetch his Winchester. It could very well be that Carter had had a simple accident. It could well be that everything would still be all right but that Carter was lying somewhere up there, injured and in need of assistance. After all, he was not that good a driver. He might just have miscalculated a rock, broken an axle; there could be a thousand innocent explanations of why the team would be standing here now at the nearest potable water. It probably was a stupid waste of time to go get the Winchester now when Charles Carter could be lying beside the Rio de las Vegas someplace upstream with a broken leg or busted ribs.

Longarm wheeled back toward the Martin house and his rifle.

Charles Carter was not lying somewhere with a broken leg, and he was in no pain whatsoever.

He lay in the bright sunshine, spreadeagled on his back, a brown stain of dried blood on the rocks under his body.

Downstream twenty or so yards the wreckage of the carriage lay half in the flow of the river, the moving water making one shattered wheel spin lazily, like a sluggish, spindly millwheel.

Longarm continued past the wreckage and past the body—Carter was beyond caring now—and rode upriver with his Winchester held ready across his pommel.

Not more than forty yards away he found what he was looking for. A boulder where the ambushers had waited. Half a dozen cartridge cases lay brass-bright in the glare of the morning sun.

The sons of bitches had given Carter no chance at all. They waited in hiding until the Zum superintendent was too close for them to miss before they fired.

Now they were long gone. Longarm stood in his stirrups and listened more than looked, his senses reaching out to the barren mountain walls on either side of the Rio.

His horse flicked its ears and stamped a foot, aware of no intrusion. Upriver a pinon jay screeched and fluttered at the approach of a magpie. Nothing else moved.

He dismounted and tied the horse to a shaft of cedar driftwood wedged against the upper part of the boulder where the ambushers had waited. Manure piles showed that other horses had been tied here quite recently. Longarm could guess whose.

The tied horses had been barefoot, he saw. No iron shoes on them. But the hooves were trimmed, the edges smooth and even.

Interesting.

He bent to examine the footprints left by the men who had waited. There were three of them, he saw. All wearing moccasins. No boots. No shoes. Moccasins.

He grunted. The message was clear...*too* clear?... this murder had been committed by Indians. Not Zuni, though. The Zuni Longarm had seen mostly went barefoot or wore sandals. Funny how he had not consciously noted that before, but it was true now that he thought on it. He brought back to mind the men he had seen at the well this morning. Sandals and bare feet. No moccasins. But then, the Zuni were not really a hunting people. They preferred weaving and pottery to leatherwork.

These men wore plains-style moccasins.

Apaches, then, of course.

Longarm smiled grimly to himself.

Sure they were Nadene.

At least they wanted someone—him—to think they were.

The assholes didn't know enough to wear the right kind of moc. The Nadene wore moccasins that had a baggy, crudely shaped foot with a sometimes decorated but usually utilitarian upper shaft of soft leather.

These imprints showed moccasins that had a slanted toe, difficult to cut and to craft but handsome and comfortable. Moccasins very much like those made by the northern plains tribes way the hell and gone north and east from here. Out of place by a good five, six hundred miles. Crow moccasins, if Longarm had to guess, although he could be wrong about that detail.

He pulled out a cheroot and took his time about lighting it. He was in no hurry to go look at Charles Carter's body. He already had too good an idea of what he would find there.

White murderers trying to lay their crimes onto Indians mostly overdid the mutilations. Scalping was rarely enough for them. They wanted to leave clues and generally didn't know when to quit. Didn't know that enough was enough.

Charles Carter's body was not going to be pleasant to handle, damn it.

There was also the question of which way to take it—

upriver or down. Up to the Zum headquarters or down to Vega Zuni.

Either way was going to cause one hell of a commotion.

At the mine, news of an Indian attack was going to mean guns and vengeance fury. He could be double-damn sure that word *would* spread, no matter what he said or did to block it.

Down among the farmers, news of Carter's death coming on the heels of the promises and all the bright hopes would mean anger and fear and hopelessness. And possibly guns there too.

Hell, the Zuni were already upset enough to start toting guns instead of hoes. He could not reasonably expect their feisty young men to quit thinking in terms of arming their Apache neighbors now.

It was something he would have to think about before he moved in either direction.

And something else he needed to work out, damn it, was, *who stood to benefit from this?*

Murders were not committed without reason.

Never.

Even if that reason was nothing more complicated than plain old insanity, there was *always* a reason. Always.

Longarm clenched the cheroot between his teeth and stared off toward the dry, gray mountaintops as if they could give him the answer.

Someone had killed Charles Carter for a reason, and that reason was not simple insanity.

Three men had waited in that ambush.

Three men do not all go mad together.

Somebody stood to benefit from Charles Carter's murder.

When Longarm figured out who that was, he would know who had butchered the superintendent of the Zuni Mountain Mining Company.

He took his time about finishing his smoke and flipped the butt into the waters of the Rio de las Vegas. His hand moved to touch his pocket, reassuring himself that his wallet and badge were still there.

When he found out who murdered Charles Carter, by

125

damn, it was within Longarm's jurisdiction to bring that bastard down. Sheriff Dewar's telegram guaranteed it.

With a grunt of disgust, he started down toward the body.

"'Lo, Longarm."

"Hello, Bennett." Longarm dismounted and tied the horse to the rail in front of the Zum office building.

"Where's Charles?"

"Didn't he make it back here last night?"

Bennett looked alarmed. "Hell, no. You mean he was s'posed to?"

Longarm nodded. "He left Vega Zuni before dark. I stayed there for the night. He said he wouldn't need any help getting home, but that wasn't necessary. On my way up this morning I found his carriage overturned and half in the river. Figured he had an accident and walked the rest of the way in. He hasn't showed up here yet?"

"No, and I been looking for him. Just checked at his house a few minutes ago. I got some bad news for him."

"Oh? What's that, Bennett?"

"I don't know as you ought to hear it before him."

Longarm shrugged.

He was more interested in trying to read Buster Bennett's face and reactions than in anything the man was saying.

If Bennett already knew that Charles Carter was dead, the man was certainly cold enough about it.

But then, a head-buster like Bennett would be. Death was not something that was new to him. He had caused enough of it in his time.

Longarm helped himself to a seat on the front edge of the porch beside Bennett and pulled out a cheroot, offering one to Bennett and lighting both of them.

He wished he had had a chance to wash his hands before he saw Bennett. He felt unclean, and no amount of rinsing his hands in the fouled water of the Rio de las Vegas had made any of that feeling go away.

It had not been pleasant burying Charles Carter's muti-lated body in the heat of the morning. The sun had been

126

wicked in the nearly airless confinement of the canyon. Burying Carter had been uncomfortable, and it was nearly as bad trying to wash his blood off the rocks. Perhaps the worst part had been trying to find Carter's scalp. It was missing, of course. One of the killers could have carried it away as a souvenir, or they might simply have tossed the bloody bit of flesh into the river. There was no way to tell. Longarm had looked for it in case the killers discarded it anywhere near, but he hadn't found it. For some reason it seemed important to him that all of Carter be buried in one place, but he just hadn't been able to find the damn scalp.

"Maybe I should send a search party down the river an' see can we find him," Bennett suggested.

Longarm shrugged again. "Do what you want. I just came up that way and I sure never saw him. Don't see how a man could get lost between here an' Vega Zuni, though. All you got to do is follow the river. A blind man could do that."

"You say he wrecked his rig?"

"That's right. It's half in the water, maybe eight, ten miles down."

"But you never seen Charles."

"Nope." Longarm pulled on his cheroot. The smoke tasted good. It helped him relax now.

"Well, if you didn't see him he ain't there. But I'd feel better to get a search party out looking for him. 'Scuse me."

"Sure."

Bennett got up and walked down toward the saloon building. He was barely gone when the secretary, Robert, stuck his head out the door and looked around.

"Why, hello, Marshal."

"Hello, Robert."

"You haven't seen the superintendent, have you?"

"Not since yesterday afternoon when we parted company down at the valley."

Robert flushed crimson above his celluloid shirt collar. "No, no," he stammered unhappily. "I . . . I mean the . . . uh . . . *new* superintendent."

"Who?"

127

"Superintendent Bennett, Marshal." Robert sighed heavily. "Mister Bennett is superintendent now. The wire came in last night. From the board of directors, sir. I . . . there's a lot of papers he has to sign. Taking responsibility for the equipment and authorizing the payroll and . . ." His shoulders slumped. "Lots of things, Marshal."

"Now, isn't that interesting," Longarm mused.

"It was . . . unexpected . . . if you don't mind my saying so, Marshal. I mean . . . Mr. Carter was a fine gentleman to work for. I feel bad for him. I've been hoping to see him this morning. To tell him right out that I feel badly about his dismissal. I . . . don't want to leave until I tell him that."

"You've been fired too, Robert?"

"Oh, no, sir. I haven't been. But . . ." He straightened his shoulders and firmed his jaw. "Frankly, sir, I don't believe I should enjoy remaining with the company after Mr. Carter's dismissal. I intend to leave as soon as possible."

"There's nothing disloyal about that, Robert." Longarm examined the ash at the tip of his cheroot for a moment. "When did you say that wire arrived?"

"I'm not sure, exactly. Some time during the night. Late, I expect, because I was here working until ten or after. There was nothing up until then except routine production reports and freight car orders for the next shipments. I'm sure of that. I always check the message traffic to see if there is anything I need to alert Mr. Carter to. That is, I did do that normally. Mr. Carter always liked to be informed of things right off. I've no idea how Mr. Bennett will wish to handle things."

"I'm sure there will be changes, Robert."

"Yes, sir. I'm afraid there will be," Carter's secretary said glumly.

"Has Mrs. Carter been told?"

"Yes, sir. Mr. Bennett was . . . quick to get the word around this morning. Mrs. Carter cried. I believe she is packing now, sir. She said something . . . well, it wasn't the sort of thing you would expect a lady to say, but . . . I was proud of her, sir. Mrs. Carter is a fine lady. As fine a lady as Mr. Carter is a gentleman. I hope they will have a happier future than this experience has been for them."

"Yes," Longarm said automatically. He felt only sadness, though. For dead Charles and for the the widowed lady who was already shattered but who did not even know yet that she was a widow. Longarm's silence was a regrettable cruelty to a lady who had given him only kindness on the one occasion when he had spent any time with her.

Damn it. Damn it all, anyhow.

"If you would excuse me now, sir, I have some things to clean up. Before I turn in my resignation. I don't want to leave anything in disorder. Mr. Carter would not want that, I know."

"Thank you, Robert. If I see Bennett I'll tell him you need some things signed up here."

"Thank you, sir."

On an impulse, Longarm stood and shook Robert's hand before the young clerk went back into the office. "Goodbye, Robert."

"Goodbye, sir."

Longarm threw his unfinished cheroot into the gravel.

Damn it all, anyhow.

Chapter 16

That answered that, then. Leon Buster Bennett was the one who profited from Charles Carter's death.

Or did he?

That message came in during the night, probably after Carter was killed.

But who the hell *knew* Carter was dead?

Whoever had killed him, of course. And whoever the killers might have told. No one else *could* know. Longarm had made sure of that himself just a few hours ago.

So that telegraph message replacing Carter with Bennett as superintendent arrived here *before* there was general knowledge that Charles Carter was dead.

He went inside the office building. "Could you help me with something, Robert? I don't want to take you away from your work, but I think this is important."

"Of course, sir. Anything I can do. Mr. Carter was quite specific about that. He instructed that you were to have our fullest cooperation."

"I need to find out what messages went out of here last night. Is there a log kept?"

"Oh, yes, sir. We keep a complete log of all traffic, incoming and outgoing. Or, of course, you could talk with the night telegrapher. He is in 'C' boarding house. I could find him for you if you wish."

"Let's not wake him just yet. The log should do to begin with." The telegrapher, Longarm recalled, would be very much in Buster Bennett's pocket. The proof of it was in Bennett's knowledge about the message Longarm received from Sheriff Dewar the other day.

"Whatever you say, sir. I should already have the file copies here somewhere."

Robert rummaged in a wire basket set at the corner of his desk until he found a thin sheaf of message forms similar to the one that lay folded inside Longarm's wallet.

"Here are copies of all the incoming traffic, sir, and..." He pulled out another bundle. "Here are the outgoing." He handed both to Longarm.

"This won't get you in any trouble, will it, Robert?"

Robert smiled at him. "Wouldn't matter much even if it did, would it, sir?"

"No, I guess it wouldn't at that."

"Mr. Bennett hasn't seen fit to give any orders about you, sir, so I shall continue to follow the last instructions I received on the subject."

Longarm winked at him and accepted the two stacks of message forms.

He helped himself to a chair near Robert's desk and went through both stacks. What he was looking for, of course, was anything that could possibly, by any stretch of the imagination, be considered a coded or shady-worded notification that Charles Carter had been murdered.

There was nothing.

Not unless someone had set something up a hell of a long time in advance of the need for it.

No double meanings. No hints. Nothing. Just dull figures reporting tonnage of ores extracted, tonnages milled, hundredweights concentrated, pounds smelted, supplies requested, hours worked... strictly routine business as far as Longarm could make out.

Except, of course, for the message naming L. Bennett superintendent of the Zuni Mountain Mining Company as a replacement for C. Carter, whose employment was "terminated forthwith."

Longarm grunted and read the message again.

Very dry, very straightforward. Signed by A. Howard, chairman, board of directors, Zuni Mountain Mining Company.

The night telegrapher had helpfully written down the time of receipt for that one as 2:17 A.M.

132

Past two in the morning, Longarm thought. Hours past the time Carter would have been dead and scalped and left lying beside the river miles downstream from here.

But how could anyone have *known* that outside of these mountains?

No one could. That was the only answer he could come up with. No one could have known.

The only wire close by was right here at the Zum headquarters. There sure as hell was none at Vega Zuni. From here . . .

"Robert."

"Yes, sir?"

"These telegraph wires. Where do they go?"

"Why, we can reach 'most anyplace you want, Marshal. Anyplace that has telegraph communications, that is."

"No, I mean these wires specifically. Where do they run?"

"Well, let me see." Robert cupped his chin in his hand and stared vacantly toward the wall. "From here specifically the wires follow the rails over Meer's Pass and out to Grants, sir. From there we have to relay, either east through Albuquerque or west again to Gallup. And, of course, to any points beyond those."

"And the company headquarters, Robert. Where would that be?"

"Right here, sir. Unless you mean the corporate headquarters?"

"Yeah, that's what I want. This form doesn't show where the message originated."

"Why, that's in Gallup, sir."

"It's local money behind the corporation, then."

"Yes, sir. Pretty much so, I believe. Was there something . . . ?"

Longarm shook his head. "No. Just grasping at straws," he admitted. "I really don't know what I mean."

Robert gave him a thin smile. "This seems to be the day for that, sir."

"Yes, doesn't it." Longarm sighed heavily and stood, returning both sets of papers to Robert's wire basket. "Thanks for your help."

"Any time, sir."

Longarm walked out into the sunshine. He sure as hell hadn't accomplished anything with that little business. Proved nothing at all except that no one here seemed to have told anyone that Carter was dead. Bennett's appointment to Charles Carter's job apparently was unrelated to Carter's murder. Longarm seriously doubted that anyone could have murdered Carter yesterday evening and gotten to a telegraph in Gallup or Grants either one in time to send that message back to Bennett.

Which pretty much chilled the half-formed theory that had been nibbling at the back of Longarm's thoughts ever since he found Charles Carter's body.

The truth of it, he guessed, was that he *wanted* the murderer to turn out some way to be Buster Bennett.

And that was damn sure no way to go about looking into a crime.

The thing was to find out who did it, not who he would like to arrest for it.

At least there was one thing he could do something about. He had missed breakfast this morning and he was hungry as hell. At least that was a matter he could solve.

He headed down toward the company buildings flanking the stinking Rio de las Vegas.

"Congratulations," Longarm said.

"You heard, eh?" Bennett was beaming with pride and pleasure. He helped himself to a seat across the table from Longarm.

"I heard." The words came out dry but even. Longarm was doing his best to keep his personal opinions out of this. Although that opinion happened to be that the Zum board of directors could not have made a worse choice for superintendent if they had deliberately set out to do so, and chosen their candidates only from lunatic asylums. Buster Bennett was one dangerous son of a bitch.

Longarm concentrated on the plate of food in front of him, poking at a tough, overcooked pork chop that was resisting his efforts to eat it. Maybe there was something to be said for hunger after all if this was the alternative.

134

"I got that search party off t' look for Carter," Bennett informed him, pulling out a fat, pale-leafed cigar Longarm recognized as being the same kind that had been in Charles Carter's humidor. It looked like Bennett was already helping himself to the things in the dead man's office. It did not, of course, necessarily follow that Bennett knew Charles Carter was dead. It could mean no more than that Bennett was rude and insensitive. Which he probably was, regardless of whatever else he knew or did not know.

"Glad to hear that," Longarm said. "I hope they find him soon. Or somebody else could've already found him and taken him in. You know. Some hunter or sheepherder or a prospector hoping to set up in competition to you boys."

"Yeah, that's true. Even coulda been some Injuns, I expect."

"Possible," Longarm said. He found it interesting that Bennett had mentioned Indians, considering the false sign that had been left by Carter's body.

"You notice any tracks while you was coming up this morning?"

Longarm shook his head. "But I wasn't looking for any. I was just covering ground and most of the time about half dozing in the saddle. You know how that is."

"Sure," Bennett agreed.

Hell, there never was a day when Deputy Long rode anywhere, not for a step, that he wasn't acutely aware of everything around him. But Bennett would not know that.

"Now that you're the superintendent here," Longarm said, changing the subject, "there's something I need to discuss with you."

"Shoot."

Don't tempt me, Longarm thought. But what he said was, "It's a plan Carter and the farmers worked out. So everybody can get along in the future and nobody get hurt doing it."

"Yeah?" Bennett at least sounded interested. He leaned forward, propping his elbows on the table that was between them. "Tell me about it."

Longarm did, trying to put into the plan some of the

135

enthusiasm and eagerness that both Carter and the men of Vega Zuni had displayed yesterday.

When he was done, Bennett frowned.

"Something wrong, Buster? It sounds like a perfect solution to me."

"O' course it does. For them pet Zuni o' yours, Longarm. O' course you'd be for it." He shook his head. "Not that I c'n imagine a businessman going for a plan like that. But then that's the reason the board had t' go an' replace ol' Charles. The man was like that, y' see. Too free with other folks dollars. Not enough sense o' loyalty to his stockholders. Things'll be different now, you can bet. I'm not gonna run the kind o' loose ship that ol' Charles did. Count on that."

No surprise there, Longarm thought. Aloud he said only, "Like I said, Buster, it makes sense to me, and it does"—he barely caught himself in time to keep from saying "did"—"to Carter too. The farmers would provide all the real labor involved. That would be the major expense. The labor, you know. The company would spend practically nothing on the project."

Bennett snorted loudly. "Practically nothing? Hell, Longarm, even without putting figures t'gether I know better'n that. Just off the top o' my head I can see that the company'd have to kick in the engineering t' design them ponds. That's expensive just by itself. An' there'd be equipment needed. That'd be the company's. An' maintenance on that stuff. An' haulage? Hell, man, you know there'd be tons an' tons of rock an' fill to haul down. An' portland to hold it all t'gether. And all of it skimmed right off the top of our operatin' expenses, right from where the profits ought to be. It'd set back our profits, why, who knows fer how long." He puffed on his cigar.

"Carter already mentioned the fill," Longarm said. "He suggested they use mine tailings for that. The tailings are already dug and loose, and they get in the way of the mining anyhow. Complete dead waste as far as the company is concerned, and no cost to anybody."

"They'd still have to be hauled," Bennett objected.

"By the farmers themselves. They are donating their time and labor and wagons, remember."

Bennett snorted again. "Haul that much fill in a bunch of little bitty farm wagons? Shit, you and me both know better'n that. We'd have to use our big ore-haulers to get the job done, and that'd come right out of the stockholders' profits." He leaned back in his chair and shook his head. "No way I'm gonna approve a stupid plan like that, Longarm. I'm sorry, but them Injuns o' yours aren't gonna get this company to pay their way. Not so long as I'm in charge they ain't. You want dams built for them red bastards, you get the gov'ment to pay the freight. Not this company. Not while I have anything t' say about it."

Longarm gave up on the pork chop and Bennett too. He pushed back away from the table. The rejection of Carter's sensible plan was no more than he had expected now that Bennett was the boss.

Dammit, though, that was personal opinion talking again. He owed those farmers down in the valley, good and decent people in all three bunches of them whatever their color and language, better than this. He tried one more time, trying to make his voice and expression as pleasant and inoffensive as he could.

"Look. Buster. Do just one thing for me. Work up some cost figures on this idea. I think you'll be surprised at how little it would cost the company. And it would give the company a world of good will with your neighbors downriver. That has to be worth something."

Bennett blinked, and then laughed at him. "Longarm, if it takes one silver dollar away from the profits o' the company, I won't even think about it. As for good will, this ain't politics, m'friend. An' I ain't running any popularity contest with a bunch of stinkin' savages. Those hoe-pounders can take their diggin' sticks an' stick 'em up their asses for all I care about their good will. An' they can stay off company property, too. You tell 'em that, Longarm. This here is private property, claimed an' filed an' recorded all legal as you please with the gov'ment of this here territory. Nobody but authorized employees of the company got any right to set a single foot on it. Or they'll get their asses

137

blown clean off their backsides. You understand me, Marshal?"

Longarm tensed but willed himself not to show it. "Does that mean me, too, Buster?"

Bennett hesitated for a fraction of a second, for so short a time that it might have been imagined although Longarm knew that it was not. Then he smiled and spread his hands wide in a show of innocence. "Hey. Don't get so hot under the collar, huh? This is a law-abidin' outfit. You're on *our* side when it comes t' that, eh? You're welcome here any time, an' you can count on full cooperation from every man here. Right?"

"Yeah," Longarm said. "Sure."

He turned away from the smiling Bennett. Already Longarm was worrying about how he was going to tell those poor sons of bitches down in the valley that they had to call off the happiness now. Charles Carter's plan for neighborliness was as dead now as Charles Carter was.

Chapter 17

After supper Longarm walked out along the river to have a smoke. The atmosphere inside the Martin house was not strained exactly, but it was a bit awkward. He and Jane had already said their goodbyes, and she had made it pretty plain that she was not prepared to un-say them. Particularly after the bad news he had brought back. Every adult in the damn valley was glum this evening.

At least Bubba and his sisters were happy. Longarm had stopped on his way down from the mines. He pawed through the gravel at the edge of the river long enough to find some of the pretty-colored stones the little girls liked to play with. And Bubba, too, even if he did try to keep from showing his pleasure. It wasn't manly to play with blocks and colors and bright stones, but he was still little boy enough to secretly treasure the stones Longarm gave him.

Longarm stood for a time staring up the river toward the mountains and the distant, unseen Zum mines.

He'd gone and made a problem for himself, he admitted silently, feeling nearly as low as the farmers after he told them the deal with Carter was off.

He had hidden Carter's body with the thought that keeping the death a secret might give him a lead to who had committed the murder.

And all right, damn it, he had been banking on the party with guilty knowledge to be Leon Bennett.

Now he'd not only failed to prove anything with this secret burial, he had gone and made it difficult to suddenly up and "find" the body.

Mrs. Carter deserved better than the double grief Longarm was giving her. First her husband fired. Now Carter missing. The lady would be in a torment of worries, and Longarm wasn't helping her a bit by delaying the last and worst blow for her. He might have done things differently if he had known, if he had thought, but ... Too late to change anything now. He had to play out the hand he himself had dealt.

He turned back toward the houses of the Anglo settlement.

Someone was moving among the homes. A man's floppy hat was silhouetted against a lamplit window. And over there another. And another?

Longarm grunted and paid closer attention.

All through the community, men had left their supper tables and were heading purposefully in the same direction. All of them walking swiftly in the direction of old Ice's place.

Not drifting along, either, the way the drinking men always did, ambling along toward the jugs Ice kept handy for them to share. Walking right along. A lot of them. And all at just about the same time, too.

It smacked of a meeting, Longarm thought, for so many to be gathering at one time.

Interesting that he hadn't been invited.

He threw his cheroot into the sour water of the Rio and moved forward himself. But unlike the farmers who were gathering, Longarm melded silently into the shadows and walked very, very softly.

"Them Mexes had the right idear," a voice claimed. "Wrong angle but the right idear. The Zums don't give a crap if we starve out. Long as they fill their pockets, it's fine by them if our women and kids go hungry. I say it's time we give the bastards something to think about."

"Won't do us any good to bust the dams," another voice cut in. "You heard what the marshal and that Carter feller said about that. Be cutting our own throats to do that."

There was a low snigger of bitter laughter. "Wasn't *our* throats I was thinking of cutting."

"Whatcha got in mind, Ben?"

Again the low laughter. "Not the dams, boys. Them

dams hold back some of the acid. Not enough of it, but some. What we got to do is stop the acids and shit from coming into our river. Then it don't make any difference if there's dams or not."

"But . . ."

"Think about it," the voice identified as Ben—Longarm could not remember which of the farmers this Ben would be—went on. "If the Zums aren't producing, they aren't pouring shit into our river." There was a short pause. "Simple."

A murmur of voices agreed with Ben.

"Hand me that jug, will ya?" Pause. "Thanks."

"Don't be greedy with that."

"Are you with me?"

"How d'you figure to do it?"

"Hell, I don't know. We'll have to think on that some. Maybe send some scouts up there. The marshal says we aren't welcome on their private, personal property, but I don't reckon there's anything wrong with putting some boys on the hilltops to look things over. Work out a plan."

"I still got some giant powder from where I had to blow rock to get my well down," a new voice said.

"So do I."

"Right. I expect most of us do. We can round up everything we got. If we need more we'll take up a collection and send a wagon to Gallup for it. Get some powder together. Meantime some of us can take a look-see up there and decide where it'd do the most good."

My oh my, Longarm thought. He was leaning casually against the back wall of Ice's cabin, not a dozen feet from the dogtrot where the Anglo farmers had gathered. He reached inside his coat to pull out a cheroot, then dipped two fingers into a vest pocket for a match. He stepped over to the back end of the open breezeway and stood facing the group of men, none of whom had yet noticed his presence there. He stood with his feet braced wide and his coat flopping open, boldly displaying the holstered Colt that rode just left of his belt buckle, slanted slightly for a cross-draw.

He struck the match and let it flare, the light of the intense flame reaching his chiseled face from below, highlighting his chin and moustache and hatbrim but keeping his eyes in deep shadow. The effect in the night, he knew, would be damn near demonic. He hoped he looked like he had suddenly appeared among them, right straight out of the pits of hell.

Someone let out a little yip of surprise, and every head in the bunch turned toward him.

Several of the men had the good grace to look sheepish. Most of them looked angry once they got over the surprise of seeing him there.

Longarm let the sulphur burn off the tip of the match, then applied the flame slowly and carefully to the tip of his cheroot, holding it there and twisting the slim stick of tobacco until he had a coal that satisfied.

Still he took his time, letting the silence grow. He blew out the match, pinched it between thumb and finger to make sure there was no flame remaining, and broke the match stem before he dropped it onto the ground. Then he glided over to the wall of the dogtrot and leaned against it with his ankles crossed in very much the same posture he had taken behind the house a little earlier.

"So far," he said slowly, removing the cheroot from his teeth and holding it out so he could examine the dull red glow of the coal, "so far you boys are liable to arrest for conspiracy to commit a felony." He looked them over one by one, locking his eyes onto theirs each in turn before he moved on to the next man and the next and the next.

"That's so far." He replaced the cheroot in his mouth and hooked his thumbs into his gunbelt. "Does anything happen up at that mine, I expect I could add felony trespass, destruction of private property, a few odds and ends beside those." He inspected the cheroot again. "And then if there's somebody inside whatever you decide to blow, we add murder if anybody dies, assault with intent to commit murder if somebody survives, both of those if some live and some don't." He took a pull on the smoke, held it deep in his lungs for a moment, and then exhaled slowly.

"What with one thing and another," he said, again looking from man to man, "I expect you could be looking at four years bottom, life tops." He smiled at them. "But that's only if somebody dies, of course. In all probability I don't expect any of you would spend more than fifteen years doing hard time." He paused. No one spoke.

"Think about that." He stood upright and partially turned, then looked back at them again. "You boys do what you want, of course. But you think about that."

Longarm jammed the cheroot back between his teeth and strode off into the darkness.

Behind him he heard a voice exclaim, "Shit!"

Longarm smiled.

This had *not* been a good day, and Longarm was weary when he rode back into the settlement.

It wasn't the simple ride up to the mines and back that was getting him down. It was . . . every damn thing else.

The look in Mrs. Carter's eyes when he delivered her husband's body to her. He just hadn't been able to keep the charade about Carter going any longer. Not with her worrying that he was lying hurt somewhere. He explained that one away by saying he disturbed a coyote that was digging at the rocks that covered the body and made the discovery out of curiosity about what the coyote was after. The missing scalp he did not try to explain, but by now the rumors would be flying at the mines about Indian attacks, he was sure. Mrs. Carter had been in too much shock to care.

And that bastard Bennett pledged the full cooperation of his security people in searching for Charles Carter's murderer among those Zuni savages. There had been laughter in the man's eyes when he said that.

Longarm knew, just plain *knew*, Bennett was behind the death.

Even if the times didn't fit on when that telegram was sent, even if Bennett's appointment as superintendent had nothing to do with the murder, Longarm believed somewhere down at gut level that Bennett was behind it.

There might be no way in the world Longarm would ever prove that to the satisfaction of a court of law.

But he sure as hell believed it.

Then there had been the news at the mine itself.

Robert was still there waiting to express his regrets to

Carter before he left. The secretary was taking Carter's death almost as hard as Mrs. Carter was. But not to so much distraction that he couldn't grumble about what was already happening to the mining operation Charles Carter had put into effect there.

Under Carter the Zum miners had been reasonably paid on a day rate, and company store prices were profitable but not beyond reason.

Already under Bennett's administration, impossible production quotas had been established, with pay deductions keyed in to the production goals. In other words, without actually saying that it was so, Bennett had already cut the pay rates. And prices for liquor, room, and board had already been increased.

Perhaps worst of all toward the problems that brought Longarm here, on his way upstream to the mines he had noticed some crumbling of the spillway of the first holding dam.

An earthen dam, no matter how well faced and how sturdily built, had to be maintained if it was to stand. Buster Bennett made it clear indeed that he had no intention of wasting company funds on the repair of dams that were of no direct benefit to the Zuni Mountain Mining Company.

Given time, perhaps no more than a matter of weeks, the water channeling into the spillway of that first dam would weaken the structure. The uppermost dam would let go, collapse, and the acid water held in the pond would sluice downstream with enough force to erode the second dam. And when it went, the third would go as well.

Within a matter of weeks, months at the most, the acid outflow from the mines would be dumped directly into the Rio de ls Vegas with no holding ponds at all between the mines and the Vega Zuni farms.

Once that happened, the valley would be dead, its soil ruined, useless for the raising of crops.

The people of the valley, white and Mexican and Zuni alike, would be as ruined as the soil they tilled.

And there was nothing Longarm could do legally to stop or even to slow Buster Bennett's seemingly deliberate stupidity.

It was that knowledge that made him feel so soul-weary when he rode up to the Martin shed and dismounted.

"Hello, Bubba," he said without spirit. He began stripping the saddle from his horse.

"Hi, Longarm. Could you help me hold the lid up on this ol' trunk, Longarm? Dang ol' thing keeps fallin' down on me."

"Sure, kid." He tossed his saddle onto the low wall separating the two tie stalls in the shed and secured the horse at the grain box, then went over to the side of the low structure and held the trunk lid for Bubba. "What are you looking for, son?"

"Mr. Hodifer asked me to see if my dad had any blastin' powder around. He needs some. I don't know why." The little boy continued pawing through the pieces of scrap leather, cans of hoof dressing, and other oddments that were jumbled into the bottom of the trunk.

"I don't think you'll find any powder in there, Bubba."

"No?" The boy straightened and brushed his hands off. "I better tell Mr. Hodifer."

"You do that, Bubba."

The kid raced away to tell this Hodifer—Ben Hodifer? Longarm wondered—there was no powder here.

Longarm moved slowly and with even more fatigue than before toward the house where Jane Martin would be cooking supper.

Bubba did not know why the powder was wanted. Longarm did. In spite of the warning he had given them last night, they were going ahead with their plan to destroy the Zum mining operation.

Regardless of law and personal risk, this had become a matter of sheer self-defense, the way the farmers would see it.

These men would rather face a deputy United States marshal than a child with an empty belly.

And, Lord help him, Longarm couldn't blame them.

That was the thing. He honestly could not blame them, nor the reactions the Zunis and the peons would have when the bitter truth reached them and they knew their backs were to the wall.

It would be fight or die then in a four-sided war with everybody up in arms.

Longarm had to do something to stop Buster Bennett before the Apache were brought into this and half the damn southwest erupted in blood and gunsmoke.

He just wished he knew what.

He walked into the Martin kitchen with his boot heels dragging and slumped into the nearest chair.

Jane's toddler came squealing and running to him, showing off the tiny handful of colored pebbles in her chubby fingers, and it was all he could do to muster a smile of appreciation for the child.

A few hours later, though, belly full and night air cool on the back of his neck, Longarm sat upright on the bank of the river and grinned.

He slapped his thigh a loud crack and jumped to his feet.

All of a sudden he wasn't feeling the least bit tired any longer.

Chapter 18

Longarm raised his arm, bringing the long procession to a halt behind him.

So that was where they were. For some time now he had been wondering where Buster Bennett's "security force" kept themselves hidden. Now he knew. A glint of sunlight reflecting high on top of the mountain showed that some-one was up there with field glasses or a telescope to keep watch on the western approaches to the Zum property.

It occurred to him now that if Ben Hodifer had tried to carry out his planned spy mission from atop the mountains, the farmers would have run smack into Bennett's spies, and the whole thing would have come a cropper right there.

Longarm waved to whoever was looking him over—by now the guards should be able to recognize him well enough—then turned around and motioned for his people to stay where they were.

No doubt Bennett's boys were confused as hell by now, although they would have thought they had their fight when they saw all the damn wagons picking their way up alongside the Rio.

The cavalcade of farm vehicles stretched downriver for three hundred yards or so. Horses, men, wagons loaded heavy with tarpaulin-covered gear.

It was quite a gathering, with whites and Mexicans and Zuni all moving together for a change. Although even now the three separate groups each tended to stick together, the whites just behind Longarm, the Mexicans in the middle, and the uncertain Zuni bringing up the rear.

It was probably the language differences that enforced

the separation, Longarm thought. All three groups sure seemed to be pulling together this time.

"We'll wait here a while," Longarm called back along the line. "Someone will come out and talk. Nobody goes past me till then. Pass it back."

There was no problem getting the word back among the English-speaking whites. From there it had to be translated by Obregon Mendez for the peons and then from Spanish to Zuni by Hank.

Longarm had had a hell of a time convincing the Zuni headman to come along in person. "We need you there, Hank. If this is gonna be legal—and we got to make it legal so there's no question about anything in the eyes of the law—you have to be there. Your young men too, of course. I can't think of any better place for those youngsters to be spending their energy than up there where I can keep an eye on 'em. But you have to be there too, Hank. Otherwise the whole house of cards could fall down in a court of law."

"It will come to that?" Hank had asked.

"Count on it. It will come to that," Longarm had assured him.

"We will win in this court of your people?"

Longarm had grinned at him. "Who knows? In fact, probably not. Not in the long run. But the first part of it is entirely legal. If you're there to make the claims on behalf of the Zuni tribe. As for the rest, once our real purpose is accomplished, good lawyers'll see to it that it takes years to settle all the fine points. That's what we're counting on. Those Zum stockholders can't afford to lose years when they aren't making any return on their money. They'll cave in quick as they see what they're up against, and we'll force 'em to go back to Carter's plan. Which is all we really want."

Hank had grunted. Longarm was not sure just how much of the explanation the headman was able to comprehend.

Enough. That was what counted. Hank understood

enough that he finally agreed to come along in this odd group and to bring his hot-headed young men with him.

The Mexicans had required less persuasion, and the Anglos none at all. As soon as Longarm told the whites what he planned, they jumped at the idea.

He really suspected that the differences lay not in any basic differences of human nature but in differences of language. He was able to get through more easily to the people who understood his words as he spoke them.

Still, the important thing was that they were here now, twenty-odd wagons and more than a hundred men, all of them patiently waiting just below the third Zum holding pond while Buster Bennett's scouts reported this "invasion" with a deputy marshal at its head.

It was dinner time—the trip up was taking much longer with the cumbersome wagons than it did on horseback—and Longarm figured they had plenty of time, so he passed the word back that the men could eat while they waited.

Actually, it took less time than Longarm would have guessed. Either Bennett had an awfully fast runner or there was some form of communication between the mountain-top guards and Bennett, perhaps by heliograph or signal flags.

However that was done, Bennett appeared in person within half an hour of Longarm's signal to the watchers overhead.

The new mine superintendent was riding at the head of a force of a dozen rifle-carrying security guards. He motioned them to stay above the middle pond and rode down alone to speak. Longarm edged his horse forward to meet Bennett.

"What the fuck is this?" Bennett demanded as soon as they were close enough to speak without shouting.

"Hello to you too, Buster. Nice day; I'm fine, thank you; good to see you again too." Longarm reached for a cheroot.

"What the fuck is this?" Bennett repeated.

"These men are about ruined, Buster. Their fields are as good as gone, and there isn't a thing the law can do about it. Some of them figure to go ahead an' pull out now. A few of them say they want to do some prospecting themselves before they decide if they stay or go. But they're all scared of crossing the private property up here. I told them I'd ride with 'em and talk to you. You have a legal right to keep them from crossing your property, of course. If you want to exercise it, I'll just tell 'em to turn around." He offered Bennett a smoke and struck a match to light both cheroots.

He shook the match out and flicked the spent stem into the greenish, scummed water of the pond. "I was hoping, Buster, that you'd be white enough to let these folks drive through your valley. You got my word, of course, there there won't be any trouble from them. I made that clear to every man of them. If they give you any trouble, I personally put the cuffs on them an' haul them up to Gallup on charges. And I wouldn't go easy on 'em."

That assurance seemed to amuse Bennett. Longarm was pledging the weight of the law on Bennett's side if there was any trouble. Bennett definitely seemed to like that.

Well, that was exactly what Longarm was counting on. It was why he had said it. Butter the bastard up. It couldn't hurt.

"Naturally," Longarm went on, "I'll expect your men to leave be. Just let these poor souls alone and let them drive through. They'll be off your property quick as they can pass through it."

Bennett smiled. "I'm a reasonable man, Longarm. Tol' you that right along, haven't I?" He waited, obviously wanting an answer.

"You have indeed, Buster. You've said right along that you operate within the law and expect to keep it that way. Far as I know, Buster, you've never lied to me about that neither." That was all pure bullshit, of course. The kind of honey that traps a fly. As far as Custis Long was concerned, Leon Bennett was a lying, cheating, murdering son of a bitch. But this would not be the best time to mention the opinion.

"Now I like you, Longarm. I surely do." Bennett smiled

grandly. "An' when I tell a man I want t' help him, I mean it. I take your word for these damn farmers, an' I give you my permission for the whole stinkin' bunch of 'em to cross comp'ny property on their way to wherever. Is that fair, Longarm? Is that fair enough?"

"Fair as a man could be," Longarm agreed. He reached forward and offered his hand for Bennett to shake. "Thanks."

"Give me just a minute to tell my boys. Don't want any trouble, we don't. You jus' let me tell my boys, and them farmers can move right on through. We won't bother 'em none. Won't even cuss 'em any where they can hear." Bennett chuckled.

Oh, he had the upper hand here, and he was loving it.

Shithead, Longarm thought silently to himself.

Longarm smiled. And thanked Bennett and thanked him.

Yessir, Buster, he was thinking. Glow and gloat all you can today. Tomorrow you're in deep shit, and I'm just the law-abiding son of a bitch to put you there.

He might never be able to prove Bennett had anything to do with Charles Carter's death.

It did not necessarily follow that Longarm was willing to forget about it.

"I'll give you, what, ten minutes before I get these farmers moving?"

"Plenty o' time, Longarm. That's plenty o' time."

"Thanks, Buster. You really can't know how much I appreciate this."

Buster Bennett smiled. So did Custis Long. They turned their horses and each rode back to his respective group, Bennett to the gunsels with their Winchesters and Longarm to his farmers with their canvas-hidden shovels and axes.

"What the hell do we do now?" Bobby asked. The man who wanted to marry Jane Martin asked the question, but the same concern was in the eyes and undoubtedly in the thoughts of every other man in the group. Those who were there. Some were still out hunting for a site that would

151

offer the unique combinations of terrain, of topography, that would allow Longarm's plan to work.

"We might have to change plans a little," Longarm admitted. The sunshine in this nearly airless canyon miles upriver from the Zum mines was brutal. He stepped gratefully under the shelter of a tarp someone had rigged as a shade and hunkered so he could draw in the dust. The farmers, all colors of them except for the Zuni who were represented only by their headman, gathered closer.

Longarm picked up a twig and used it to sketch the course of the Rio de las Vegas as far as they had already followed it.

"What I was looking for," he said, "like I told you already, was a place where we could divert the whole damned river. Well, from where I sit, we aren't gonna be able to do that. Not without pulling down half a mountain range, we aren't. And if we had time and money enough to do that, well, there wouldn't really be enough of a problem to make it worthwhile going through with it anyhow."

The farmers looked worried. Hopeless. Once again it seemed Longarm had raised new hopes only to have those hopes dashed at the last moment, just as the excitement of Charles Carter's plans had been proven false.

The Anglos showed their concern first, their faces falling as Longarm spoke. Then the peons, who had to wait for Mendez's translation before they frowned. Hank's broad, stoic face showed no changes. But then, Hank had not looked hopeful to begin with.

"I been thinking, though," Longarm went on. "Maybe we don't have to divert. Maybe it will work just as good if we build on the flimsy side to begin with. Deliberately. Hold the river, not divert it. Hold the flow just long enough, then deliberately blow a gap and let everything down at once. I don't know how long we could block it before the water backed up and we had to worry about an overspill. I just don't know about that. A week, two weeks, maybe a few days longer. I just don't know."

Mendez said something to one of his men, and the peon jumped up and ran toward the river, standing with his back

152

to the rest of the men and staring as if in concentration. His head kept bobbing like he was muttering something to himself. Longarm ignored the momentary distraction.

"Anyway," he said, "we could still have the same impact on them. We might have to do a lot of building and tearing down. But I still think it could work. Think about it. If we can block the river except for, oh, one day out of ten, that should be enough. The mines can't operate without water to fuel their steam engines and water to carry the crushed ore through those flumes. Water is the whole basis of their operation. They can't work without it. And if we can keep them from getting it but once every ten days or so—"

He was interrupted again when the Mexican peon came trotting back from the river bank and spoke loudly and long to Mendez.

Obregon Mendez was smiling broadly when the peon was done. Mendez turned to Longarm. "One day in eighteen, *señor*."

"What's that?"

Mendez repeated the figure.

"You sound sure."

"But I am, *señor*. Hector there is . . ." He shrugged. "Different. Eh? Slow some ways. You know?"

Longarm nodded.

"But Hector sees some things. I don' know how. Puts them together. Somehow. He looks at *el rio*. He looks at this place. He says to me if a wall is made so high—" Mendez gestured with his palm to a point about at a level with his hairline—"the waters will not spill for eighteen days. Do not ask me how he knows. He knows." Mendez shrugged again.

Longarm grinned. "All right. We'll take his word for that. It can't be any worse than a guess I could make. We'll figure eighteen days' hold-back. Now, you boys think about that. If the Zums can only operate their mine once every eighteen days, how much profit do you figure they could make? None, that's how much. And those boys are down there to make a profit, pure and simple. They got payrolls to meet and expenses to pay and investment to recover. They can't do any of that if they can only mine one day out of eighteen. Right? So we shut their water off up here, and we've got them in a position where they *got* to bargain. Then you just tell them you'll drop *your* mining plans if they agree to go with Charles Carter's plan. Right?"

The farmers were grinning again. Even the impassive Zuni grunted with a sound that might have been satisfaction.

The "mining plans" Longarm spoke of were only an excuse for the farmers of Vega Zuni to build a dam of their own.

But it would be legal, by damn.

It would be legal as all billy hell. And that was what counted.

"Do we go with it?" Longarm asked.

"Damn right," Ben Hodifer swore.

"*Sí.*"

Hank nodded slowly. He looked solemn.

"That's it then, boys," Longarm said, standing but having to remain hunched over so his Stetson did not bump into the tarp that was providing the shade. "I think it would be appropriate if the honors of staking out this mining claim, in the name of the Zuni nation, under the mineral and mining laws of the United States of America, was shared by everybody. What d'you say?"

There was a cheer, joined quickly by the peons even before Mandez had time to translate the words. And this time even Hank smiled.

Longarm bent and picked up a handful of pebbles that he and the men had gathered earlier. The worthless, prettycolored things were strewn virtually the whole length of the Rio de las Vegas. They were useless, of course, except for play-pretties that children liked. Or possibly as ornamental color that could be set into silverwork. Like, say, the kind of bracelets and necklaces and doodads the Zuni silversmiths made.

Longarm laughed out loud.

154

Stupid, worthless pebbles. But because they were in the stream, and because the Zuni made jewelry, there was absolutely nothing in the mining and mineral laws of the country that said they couldn't stake a claim for the recovery of red and blue and green pebbles, just as claims were staked for the recovery of gold and silver and lead.

The law, after all, didn't say how valuable the minerals had to be. Or who the stuff was valuable to. Just that the claimed minerals were present and of value.

So there was just nothing at all to keep the Zuni from staking out a claim on the Rio de las Vegas so they could mine stones for their jewelry production.

And that, by damn, was exactly what they were going to do. All legal and aboveboard. And since the Zunis would hold the claim rights, Deputy Marshal Custis Long and the full weight of the U.S. government would stand behind the Indian tribe's right to their claim.

Longarm laughed again. Buster Bennett wanted to stay inside the law? Fine. That was just *exactly* what they were doing here. Staying in the law.

Bennett and his Zums could use the waters of the Rio de las Vegas for their mining? Hank and Zuni and their farmer helpers could claim use of those exact same waters for *their* mine.

For their *pebble* mine.

"Something funny, Marshal?"

"Yeah. Bennett's face when he looks out his window and sees there isn't a river out there any more. That's gonna be just about the funniest thing I can think of." He looked around. "Let's get at it, boys. We got to lay out the claim and put stakes up, then send Hank and party off to Gallup to get the mine claim filed and recorded, everything on the up-and-up, you know."

Grinning, the farmers scattered to begin gathering stones for the rock cairns that would mark the corners of the claim and stones for another cairn to mark the "discovery" site where the valuable colored pebbles were located.

Once the "mine" was claimed and the dam built across the river, Buster Bennett and the Zuni Mountain Mining Company would be over the proverbial barrel. They would give in to what the farmers needed or the Zums would be plumb out of the mining business. Legal and proper, Longarm and the farmers had the mine cold. The Zums would play or fold. They wouldn't have any other choices.

Chapter 19

Longarm smiled and puffed on his smoke. Things were moving along, all right. Less than a week here, and already the dam across the Rio de las Vegas was taking shape.

They had established a camp that was really almost a small, multilingual community, and after just this short a time he was sure he could see some blurring of the separations among the three different groups. Except, perhaps, with the young Zunis since Hank had left to file and record the mining claim.

The Zuni youngsters, isolated both by background and language, were shy and kept mostly to themselves. They were workers, though. Longarm had to give them that. They did not shirk any task assigned to them and had been put in charge of gathering and stockpiling the clay that would be made into a mud and plastered over the surfaces of the dam as soon as enough aspen poles had been brought down ready to lay.

The dam construction would be pretty much an overgrown version of a beaver dam. Simple, quick, cheap, and amazingly efficient. Old, abandoned beaver dams on the mountain streams from here north into Canada could attest to the holding power of those seemingly crude structures.

And since the thing would have to be deliberately breached every now and then to keep the whole thing from being washed away by the forces of nature—much more powerful than anything the Zums could throw against them—it only made sense to do this as simply and as cheaply as possible.

Peons and farmers alike had teamed up in combinations that had more to do with the jobs a man felt comfortable with than with the language he spoke, and some odd friendships were growing as for the first time these men worked side by side on a project of common interest. Everyone chattered suggestions and encouragement in his own tongue, and it was surprising how quickly the Anglos were picking up words of Spanish and how rapidly the peons were learning English.

He looked up the valley, half hoping to see Hank and Hodifer and Rodriguez returning from Gallup with the recorded claim. They could get back any time now.

Instead of the light wagon they had driven, though, he could see only the bustle of the construction effort. The Zunis were using Mexican carts to haul clay from the pockets that had been discovered nearby. The peons and farmers were busy freighting cut timbers down from the mountainsides. The wood-cutting crews high on the surrounding slopes were busy with axes and saws providing the main material for the dam.

Closer to where Longarm stood lay the camp. Brush arbors, canvas shelters, even a few actual tents to house the workers. In the middle of it all was the fire, kept constantly burning and with an ever-hot coffee pot ready for any man who was hungry or thirsty or simply wanted a break from the labors. The cooking was being done by a peon who had had the bad luck to get in the way of a falling aspen the first morning of work. His shoulder was still sore, but the man refused to stay idle and so was assigned the cooking fire.

"How's it coming, Bobby?" Longarm called as the farmer guided a mule team in, the team dragging in several long, spindly aspen trunks. Behind Bobby, Burl Evans was bringing a wagon load of slash, the small branches trimmed from the felled tree trunks. The slash would be needed as filler material between the trunks when the dam was assembled.

"Good, Longarm. Comin' right along." He did not slow his mules or alter their course toward the now-massive stacks of timber and slash and mud that lay on both banks of the Rio.

Soon there would be material enough to begin the work of actually constructing the temporary dam.

"*Señor* Longarm?"

Longarm turned to see a dark-eyed and handsome Mexican boy of sixteen or so running toward him from downstream, where a crew was cutting willows for more filler slash.

"Yeah, Raphael?" He smiled at the kid, a nice boy, always pleasant.

Raphael stopped in front of him, gasping for breath after the running and searching for the unfamiliar English words. After a moment he gave up and pointed.

Longarm looked down the canyon but could see nothing. With an impatient shake of his head, Raphael took Longarm by the sleeve and tugged him over to the side so that the roof of a tarpaulin shelter no longer blocked his view.

"Oh." With a frown, Longarm threw his cheroot away and began walking down to greet the visitors.

There were men riding in, a bunch of them, although it was difficult to see how many in all the dust they were raising.

It was not hard to guess who the men would be.

Bobby left his mules and ran to Longarm's side. "We'll be backin' you, Longarm."

"Don't even think about it. You boys leave your shotguns be. You hear me, Bobby? And pass the word to the others. You all of you leave be. I'll handle it. Everybody else just keep on with your work. And don't anybody, I mean *any*body, show a gun."

"If you say so."

"I say so. Find Mendez. Make sure he passes that word too. No guns, no scythes, nothing. Right?"

"Right." Bobby trotted away.

Raphael was still following. Longarm motioned for him to go with Bobby. They didn't need excitement right now. Not anyone's.

Longarm walked out thirty yards or so from the camp and stood waiting for Bennett and his men to arrive.

Longarm counted eleven as they came closer at an easy jog. Bennett was leading, riding tall and sassy on a glossy black with a thick stallion neck. They passed the party of willow choppers without a sideways glance, the peons stopping their work and staring after the arrogant gunmen who had so recently murdered six Mexicans. One of the peons hefted the machete he had been using to cut the willow, and for a moment Longarm was afraid the man was going to break. But he did not. He only stood and stared at the receding backs of the gunnies.

The "security" patrol came on, coming to a halt finally just in front of Longarm. They were a well-armed crowd, each man with a repeating carbine across his pommel and at least half of them carrying spare revolvers in holsters slung from their saddle horns. They had enough firepower to fight a war and looked like they would welcome an excuse to turn loose some of that power.

"Morning, Buster," Longarm drawled.

"What the fuck is goin' on here, Longarm?"

"I said good morning, Buster."

"And I said . . . oh, shit, all right. Good morning, Longarm."

Longarm nodded. "Step down, Buster. Join me for some coffee?"

"No, I don't want any damn coffee. I want to know what the fuck's going on here." He did dismount, though. He tossed his reins to his nearest tough and came over to stand before Longarm.

He was a big son of a bitch. Bull-like build, too. Longarm suspected Buster Bennett would be a handful in a fair fight. And he suspected as well that Buster Bennett didn't fight fair. Longarm grinned at him.

"I asked you what the fuck is goin' on here."

"So you did, Buster. And I expect I'll tell you. But even if you don't want some coffee, I do. Leave your boys here and trail along with me."

Bennett grunted but motioned for his gunmen to remain where they were. He and Longarm walked toward the fire.

"What this is," Longarm said easily, "is a mining claim."

Bennett snorted loudly. "That's a fuckin' laugh. If there was mineral here our people woulda found it. There ain't a

160

showing o' gold or silver or anything like that anywhere closer'n our property."

"That's right," Longarm said agreeably.

"You can't prove a claim without a showin', dammit. I know that much."

"Of course you do," Longarm agreed. "So do I. Got to observe the legalities, right, Buster?"

"You damn well bet you do."

"And so they are." Longarm smiled and veered closer to the river. He hunkered beside the clean, flowing water and dabbled in the loose grave at its edge.

"I don't know what you're up to, but—"

"Oh, I'm not up to anything. This claim is filed by the Zuni nation. As an officer of the government of the United States, I'm only interested because the Zunis are wards of the government. My only interest in this is to see that their rights are protected."

"I'll protect their fucking rights. They can't file any claims where there ain't mineral. That's the law, mister, an' you're sworn to foller that law."

Longarm smiled and plucked a dark red pebble out of the streambed. He held it up for Bennett to see. "Mineral, Buster."

"What the hell is this? It ain't ore. Hell, it ain't even turquoise or any o' that namby-pamby shit."

Longarm shrugged. "Damned if I'd know what it is. Looks like a rock to me. Valuable to the Zuni, though. They use such stuff decorating their silver work. And some of that silver stuff they make has religious significance to them. Not that I understand it. But that piece of rock is valuable to them, and it's sure as hell a mineral. So I expect they got a right to file a claim and mine the stuff, same as you and your company got a right to file a claim and mine gold and whatever else you're producing down there. A right which, by the way, I am sworn to protect. Yours just as much as theirs."

Bennett scowled at the pebble and threw it down, wiping the grit and water on his fingers onto his trousers.

"You're up to something, you bastard."

Longarm stood. His expression had become cold.

161

"Aw, I didn't mean nothing," Bennett said before Long-arm could speak. "You know that."

"What I'm up to," Longarm said slowly, "is seeing that the peace is kept and everybody's rights are preserved. Right?"

"Yeah. Right." Bennett sounded unhappy. He knew damn good and well that Longarm was up to something, but apparently he had not quite yet worked out just what that was.

Dumb, Longarm thought.

"We didn' know..." Bennett said lamely.

"That's right. You didn't know. Now you do."

"These damn greasers an' all..."

"The Mexican-American *citizens* here, Buster, just like the white American citizens, are employed by the Zuni nation to help in the development of this here legally filed and recorded mining claim. Right?"

"Uh, yeah. Sure."

"Which means they got every right to be here too. Right?"

"Sure, Longarm. Whatever you say."

"You want to see the claim stakes, Buster? There's one right over there. And another back there. And two more, up there and there." He pointed.

"I don't need to see them. Your word is good with me, Longarm. You know that."

"And you know, Buster, that any trouble on this mining claim, anything directed against any of the Zuni or any of their employees, why, that trouble would be in violation of federal statutes. You do know that, don't you, Buster?"

"Sure. Sure, Longarm. I know that." He smiled. "But, hey, we never come up here t' give anybody trouble. We was just ... lookin' around. You know?"

"Sure, Buster. You were just looking around."

"That's it exactly," Bennett said. "This here is all within the law. We was just curious. Wanted to make sure that it was. But you know me, Longarm. Always stand behind the law, I do. You can count on that."

"Count on it? Buster, I expect to see to it."

"Uh, look, Longarm, you go on an' have your coffee

162

now. Me and my boys'll go back now. Now that we know everything's on the up-an'-up here. You know?"

"I know, Buster. I just hope you do."

"Hey!" Bennett spread his palms in a show of innocence. "I never run against the law, Longarm. Never."

"Right," Longarm said coldly.

"Well, I'll see you later."

"I hope so, Buster. I certainly hope so."

Bennett turned and headed back to his horse and his waiting gunmen. He mounted quickly and, without saying a word to any of his men, turned and headed back down the river toward the Zum mines.

Longarm watched them out of sight. He felt no particular satisfaction, though. Buster Bennett was the kind of greased snake who preferred to cloak himself in the respectability of law when he did his dirty work. But it was damned dirty work that the man did for his living. Longarm was sure this business with the Zums was not yet over and done with.

In fact, he *hoped* it was not yet over and done with.

Longarm still had a score he would like to settle with Leon Buster Bennett on behalf of Charles Carter and six dead Mexicans whose names Longarm did not even know.

The Zum plug-uglies rode away without a lick of trouble, though, and were soon lost to sight down the canyon.

Chapter 20

The dam—really little more than a brush pile laid from one wall of the canyon to the other, with sticks and mud piled in for good measure—was nearly finished. The wings on either side of the river had been built first. Now the central portion inside the river flow was being completed. The farmers had brought in the aspen saplings and planted them butt-down in the mud. The peons weaved light slash between the trunks, and now the Zunis were plastering it all with thick clay.

"Huh," Hodifer grunted with satisfaction. He pulled out his pipe and tobacco pouch and offered the tobacco around.

Hank stood with his arms folded and a look of grim satisfaction on his face.

Rodriguez, an unofficial leader of the Mexicans, said something too softly for Longarm to hear.

The waters of the Rio de las Vegas slowed to a trickle and began to back up behind the wide, low dam.

Then the trickle dropped off to nothing more than scant seepage as the young Zuni men completed their clay plastering, standing calf-deep on the water side of the new dam.

"Now what happens?" Hodifer asked.

"I figure in another few hours we'll be getting a visit from your neighbors," Longarm said. "This calls for a celebration, gentlemen. I have a bottle in my bag. Been saving it for a special occasion since there wasn't enough to share around. I think this might be a good time to drag it out."

Amusement glinted in Hank's dark eyes, but neither he

nor Longarm voiced the fact that it was entirely illegal for any white man to give liquor to an Indian.

Longarm went to fetch his bottle of Maryland rye.

"You bastards! You sons of unnatural bitches! You—"

"You're trespassing," Longarm said calmly.

"What right've you got . . ."

"All the right of the U.S. government," Longarm replied mildly. "Which we already discussed once, Bennett." He looked past the red-faced, furious mine superintendent to the gun-carrying men who were backing him.

"Figure to turn your dogs loose, Buster? Hell, there's enough of them that they might be able to take me. You wouldn't know about it, of course. You'd be dead. But they might get lucky. 'Course, they wouldn't be so lucky afterward. The Justice Department doesn't much cotton to folks who shoot it out with federal officers. But you do what you think is best, Buster."

Bennett was about to explode with wrath. His neck corded with tight-pent emotions, and his fists knotted.

But Buster Bennett was a bully, not a gunman, and if he wanted to open this ball there was no way he could take Longarm before the lean deputy put him down first, no matter how many men were behind him. Longarm was in front of him. Buster Bennett would have a belly full of lead before he ever had time to hear the gunshots. He probably knew that quite as well as Longarm did.

"What I suggest you do," Longarm said pleasantly, "is to have your lawyers look into this. Not that I really expect that would change anything. The Zuni got a copy of your claim filings and used that as a model when this one was recorded." Longarm smiled. "You see, they have faith in your lawyers. They figured they couldn't do any better than those boys did. So I kinda suspect your lawyers will find everything was done right and proper with this one too."

"You put 'em up to this, you son of a bitch."

"Doing my job," Longarm said. "Advising wards of the government. And, Buster. I'm getting a leetle bit tired of

166

your mouth. I believe I've mentioned that to you before. You really ought to keep that in mind."

"You . . . you . . ." He seemed unable to come up with anything powerful enough to meet the occasion.

"Try me or get out. You're still trespassing."

Beet-red from a fury he could neither control nor vent, Bennett whipped his horse around with a vicious yank of the reins and spurred the animal into a run.

"I think," Longarm said softly as the leaders of the three groups of farmers came up behind him, "that I'll want to sleep close to the dam for a spell. Just in case."

Two days passed without incident. Longarm slept in fits and snatches, bedding down at the base of the still filling dam while the bed of the Rio de las Vegas dried and cracked below the blockage.

During the day, the Zunis and their "helpers" made a show of digging gravel out of the exposed river bed, washing and sorting the colored pebbles, and piling the sorted stones in jumbles of rock separated by color, greens and reds and blues and whites. Longarm had no idea what the different kinds of stones were. They were all pebbles to him. For sure, though, the children of Vega Zuni would be tickled after this. The kids would have all manner of pretties to play with.

The longer they went with no open confrontation from the Zums, the more tense and worried the farmers were becoming.

Men who were supposed to be digging gravel for sorting leaned on their shovels and stared down the canyon in the direction of the Zum mines.

Longarm posted sentinels on the mountaintops to either side of the dam not only to watch for the approach of Bennett's security people but also to guard against dynamite attacks from above. The precaution did little to relieve the anxiety that was building in the camp.

On the morning of the third day, Longarm saddled his horse and slid his Winchester into the saddle scabbard.

"I'm going to ride down and pay your neighbors a

167

visit," he said. "I'll bet the telegraph wires've been hot the past couple days. Maybe I can get an idea of what they figure to do."

"You want some of us to go with you?" Ben Hodifer offered.

"Lord, no. That's the last thing that'd help." He swung onto the horse.

"But what if . . ."

Longarm smiled down at the worried man. "If I don't come back by dark, I suggest the whole crowd of you pull out and get under cover. And send somebody larruping for Gallup. Put the word out there to the sheriff and the BIA and send a wire to my boss that I've been killed in the line of duty. Send the message to William Vail, U.S. Marshal, at the Federal Building, Denver. You got that, Ben?"

Hodifer nodded unhappily. "William Vail in Denver."

"That's right." Longarm smiled. "But I don't expect you to need the information."

"Lordy, I hope not."

"If anything happens while I'm gone, don't fight back. Just get the hell out of the way. I'll take care of the rest of it, no matter what they might get up to. Remember, boys, you got the law on your side now. Just keep that in mind, and you'll be all right."

"If you say so." The farmers looked and sounded unconvinced.

"I'll be back after dinner," Longarm said. "Hell, maybe I can talk Bennett into inviting me for a meal at a table I can set down to for a change, while you fellas are back here squatting on the ground to eat and crapping in catholes." He grinned at them and rode down the canyon.

Within a quarter of a mile even the dampness caused by seepage from the base of the dam had disappeared, and the entire river bed was dry and baking in the sun.

Sure were a lot of pebbles there to pick over, he thought.

There was quite a state of confusion when Longarm rode into the Zum grounds. It looked like somebody had kicked an anthill, and all the occupants were out and running in circles.

He stopped near the shed that served as a railhead and stood in his stirrups to get a better look down the narrow valley.

Not only were men streaming down from the tunnel mouths, the equipment he could see was different from the last time he passed through here too.

Pipe had been laid from down at the holding pond end of the property, and he could see a huge boiler and steam engine down there mounted on skids. The pipe ran from the holding pond up to the mines by way of the steam engine, so the machinery pretty much had to be a pump.

Longarm frowned. Obviously Buster Bennett thought he had found a way to outsmart Longarm's suspension of the Zum water supply. Bennett was going to pump water out of the holding ponds and use that for the basic water needs of the operation. Probably just in the steam boilers. There would not be enough water impounded in those three ponds to continue transporting the ore in a slurry mixture. But ore could be carried in other ways so long as the machinery to dig it was able to operate.

"Damn it," Longarm muttered. This stopgap plan of Bennett's just might work.

And if the farmers could hold Bennett's feet to the fire long enough to make him agree to build the additional settling ponds that were needed, Longarm's whole plan was just so much smoke and wasted sweat.

"What was that, mister?"

"Huh? Oh. Sorry. I didn't see you there."

The man had been lounging just inside the railhead shed, and Longarm had not noticed him until he moved. Now he came out onto the platform and took a look down the valley at all the men coming down the hillsides. He shook his head.

"What's this all about, anyway?" Longarm asked.

The man shook his head again. "Stupidity, that's what it is."

"I don't understand."

169

"I tried to tell the idiot, but he wasn't listening." The man shook his head sadly.

"You tried to tell who? About what?"

"Mmm? Oh, that." He shook his head. "You'd be the federal man, right?"

"That's right. Custis Long, deputy U.S. marshal."

"Arlen Bates." Bates came closer and reached up to shake. "Former foreman here. Until that idiot Bennett fired me." He hesitated, then smiled. "Come to think of it, maybe it isn't a bad thing that he did. At least this way they can't hold me responsible."

"Responsible for what, Mr. Bates?"

"Why, for all this, of course." He waved in the general direction of the miners who were still busily evacuating the tunnels. "I passed the word for the boys to get out, you know. Bennett swore he'd fire me, and he did that. But I don't care. Better to lose a job than to cost good men their lives."

"I hope you will forgive me, but I have no idea what you are talking about, Mr. Bates."

Bates looked up at him, then shook his head again. Longarm could not decide if the man was expressing a thought about Longarm's ignorance or was still deploring whatever it was he deplored here.

"I'll tell you the same thing I told Superintendent Bennett, Marshal. Same thing Superintendent Carter would have said too. Mark my words about that, sir. Superintendent Carter never would have issued such foolish instructions."

"I don't . . ."

"I know, I know. You don't follow me. Well, Mr. Bennett didn't neither." Bates sighed. "Simple, really. The man plans to use water outa that pond down there to fuel his steam lifts and power the pneumatic pumps and all that, right?"

"So I would gather," Longarm agreed.

"Stupid," Bates declared. "Murderous. That's the thing. Those engines blow up, why, there's no telling who could get hurt. Probably not him, though. It'd only be justice if it was him that got blew up with the machinery, but it won't

170

be. Things never work out like that, you know. It'd be good, honest working stiffs that got hurt. That's why I told them all to get out."

"You say the engines will blow up? Why would that be?"

Bates gave him a sour look as if he thought anyone should know the answer to that one. "What's in that pond they're pulling the water from, Marshal?"

"Water, of course. Waste water."

"That's right," Bates said. "Waste water. Waste water carrying sulphuric acid and who knows what else, right?"

"Sure."

"And what happens when you let any sulph acid into a boiler, Marshal?"

"Hell, it boils, I expect."

"Ha! That's what Superintendent Bennett said too. I know better. Mr. Carter, he woulda known better. That's why Mr. Carter was a good superintendent, and that's why Mr. Bennett isn't."

"All right, Mr. Bates. What does happen when you put acid in a boiler?"

"Son of a bitch blows up, Marshal. That's exactly what will happen."

"That pump engine down there seems to be working all right," Longarm observed.

Bates cackled gleefully. "Sure it is, Marshal. Working just fine. But that boiler was already full of clean water when they sledded it down there. They haven't added any acid to it. If they do, Marshal, it'll blow too. Mark my words, sir, that one or any other they put that pond water into, it'll blow for sure."

"You're sure of that, Mr. Bates?"

"Damn right I am. But Mr. Bennett says I'm crazy. Well, let him fire up those boilers in the lift houses. He'll see how crazy I am." Bates folded his arms and stared down the valley.

The swarm of men leaving their shift had slowed to a trickle, and a group of men dressed in much cleaner clothes—Bennett's gun-handy boys, Longarm guessed—were replacing them inside the lift sheds.

171

"Just wait. You'll see," Bates said.

The miners gathered near the boarding houses, Longarm saw, but no one was going inside. They were all staring up toward the mine openings where the steam engines had been placed.

"They're gonna do it," Bates said. "Those idiots are gonna do it."

Longarm could see Bennett's guards working with wrenches to connect hoses or some kind of fittings from the water pipes to the storage tanks. He guessed that those tanks fed the boilers to make the steam than drove the equipment in the mines.

"Won't be but a few more minutes, Marshal, and those . . ."

Bates's estimate of the time remaining was short just a bit.

From a lift house to Longarm's right there was a short whuff of dull noise, and the walls of the building bulged outward. Then walls and roof alike collapsed, and chunks of steel and lumber and steam shot high into the sky.

"See?" Bates asked. He almost sounded pleased.

To the left another structure exploded, the sound of this one sharper and louder, the steam and debris flying even higher than the first had gone.

"See?"

Another boiler blew and then another.

From inside one of the tunnel openings there was a gout of steam and smoke and dust, although the noise from inside was very faint.

"Oh, my," Bates muttered. "The lift donkey in Number Four, that woulda been. I sure hope nobody was left down below. It's a long and nasty climb on the safety ladder."

Another explosion erupted, and then another.

Half the valley was obscured by dust and steam. Halfway up the mountainside a lift house had caught fire and the dry wood was blazing furiously.

"Sure used to be a nice little operation here," Bates said. "When Mr. Carter was running it. Sure did like working for that man." He laughed. "Looks now like I didn't lose so much by getting fired, doesn't it?"

172

"I would have to agree, Mr. Bates."

Down along the dry riverbed where both shifts of miners had gathered there was excitement now but no panic. The men actually seemed interested in watching the destruction that surrounded them.

Longarm had to admit it was interesting. As far as he could see there was only one building remaining on the mountainside, and it was just a small shack, probably a powder magazine, sitting off by itself away from the tunnel openings.

Even as he watched, the flimsy-legged slurry flumes, damaged at their upper ends by the force of the explosions, began to collapse, the failure of the struts starting high near the tunnels and rolling downhill with a continuous roar, like a gigantic string of dominoes falling, falling, falling all the way down the slopes on both sides of the valley.

The processing mill at the bottom of the canyon was unharmed. Apparently its boilers had held only fresh water too. And the boarding houses, store, whorehouse, office building, and superintendent's quarters were untouched.

Everything else seemed to have been blown to hell and gone, although from outside the tunnels it was possible to see little but dust and the debris of the lift houses.

"Well, I'll be go to hell, Mr. Bates."

Bates chuckled. "Glad that train's late. I wouldn't have missed seeing this for anything."

"Something tells me that your Mr. Bennett is going to be pissed about this."

"Pissed? He'll be lucky if the owners don't have him strung up. All that money shot to hell and gone now."

"They'll be able to reopen, won't they?"

Bates shrugged. "If somebody wants to spend it all the second time, maybe. Cost a bitch of a lot. And no telling what's been done to the shoring in those tunnels or how many shafts just up and collapsed. Be a bitch, I tell you. And on top of that, you see, the pay here was all right, but nothing special. If it was my money I don't know as I'd want to try again. A guy might make out or he might not. You just never know. It's like that with mining, Marshal. All you know for sure is what you got in your hand. The

173

next stroke of the pick or the next shot in the hole and your vein could pinch out and the pay be all gone." Bates chuckled again. He sounded like he hoped the company's veins would pinch out and leave them with nothing for their troubles now that he'd been fired.

As a final statement on the whole thing, down by the upper holding pond the engine that was powering the water pump exploded in a great burst of steam and flying steel. It took several seconds for the sound of the explosion to travel the length of the canyon to where Longarm and Bates were watching.

Bates threw his head back and laughed.

"If you'll excuse me, Marshal, I think I'm going to duck out of sight here again before Mr. Bennett sees me. I don't much think Mr. Bennett is the sort to admit a mistake, and I'd rather not be in his way the rest of today." Bates was laughing when he went back inside the rail shed.

Longarm pushed his Stetson back off his forehead and sat on the horse just marveling at all the damage that Leon Bennett had accomplished.

Chapter 21

Longarm was laughing when Bennett saw him. It was probably that fact that set off Bennett's rage.

In truth, Longarm was not laughing at Bennett's folly, and certainly not at the big man's disheveled condition. He was laughing at a joke one of the miners had just told to another man. Most of the miners were already trooping toward the railhead with their bundles and bags, ready for the next outbound train to arrive and assuming that their jobs here had vanished in the boiler explosions.

Bennett could not have known that, though. He saw Long, and the deputy was laughing.

Bennett was in rocky shape after the explosions. The right side of his head was steam-burnt, already red and swelling with blisters. He had a blood-caked gash in one arm from where some flying debris had struck him. And his mood was vicious.

"You son of a bitch!" he bellowed. "This is your fault."

Bennett started toward Longarm with his hands in fists, then stopped, reeling slightly. He must have known that he was in no shape to take Longarm on.

He gave a roar of frustration, turned to one of the security guards who was trailing behind him, and grabbed the man's Winchester.

"Don't," Longarm barked.

Buster Bennett was beyond listening. He fumbled with the lever, cursed, and finally got the action to function. He jacked a cartridge into the chamber of the rifle.

"I won't tell you again, Bennett. Drop it. Now!"

Bennett acted as though he did not even hear. Tears of fury welling wetly in his eyes, he raised the Winchester.

Longarm's Colt spat lead and fire. The slug took Bennett in the chest, sending the big man reeling.

Bennett was no quitter, though. He caught himself and managed somehow to remain upright, swaying and staggering but somehow maintaining his feet.

He tried once again to level the Winchester.

"Don't, damn you!"

The warning was no good.

It required all Bennett's waning strength to hold the muzzle up. He was straining. His knees wobbled and should have buckled, but he refused to drop.

Bennett brought the barrel of the Winchester level.

Longarm shot him again, taking deliberate aim this time, squeezing off the round with care.

The bullet smacked into Bennett's forehead.

Even then, already dead, Bennett tried to remain upright. His finger jerked closed on the trigger, sending a .44-40 slug harmlessly into the gravel at his feet.

Only then did his muscles give in, and he collapsed face forward in a heap.

"Jesus," someone whispered.

The security men who had been with Bennett stared at their dead chief, then at Longarm.

"Don't push it," Longarm told them. "There've been enough mistakes made here today."

"No, sir," one of the men said.

Longarm waited until he was sure the guards were no threat, then he reloaded his double-action Colt and slid it back into its leather.

"I guess," he said, "somebody needs to get some wires off to Gallup."

No one else seemed inclined to send the messages, so Longarm walked up the hill toward the Zum offices.

There would be investigations, he knew. Inquiries and possibly inquests. A whole lot of paperwork and probably lawsuits and who knew what all else. It was not a pleasant prospect.

That bothered him more than Buster Bennett's death, though.

All the way up to the office building he kept thinking

about Charles Carter, and how much better things could have been for everyone if Carter had only lived.

Longarm felt morally certain—not legally certain, of course, but morally so—that Carter's murderer was now dead and gone. It was something neither Longarm nor anyone else would ever prove, but he was sure of it.

He let himself into the empty Zuni Mountain Mining Company offices and went to the file cabinet behind Carter's—Bennett's—desk. The first thing he had to do was figure who in hell to notify about this mess. Then maybe he could wash his hands of it and go tell the farmers of Vega Zuni that they would not have to worry any longer about the Zums.

It was odd, though, how little pleasure there was in knowing he could say that now.

Longarm let himself into the sheriff's office. Dewar was there, seated behind his desk. He was alone today.

"Long." He nodded.

"Sheriff," Longarm greeted him. He removed his Stetson and took the chair in front of the desk.

"You played hell down there, didn't you, son?"

Son. It wasn't all that often that anyone called him son any more. Coming from Dewar, somehow Longarm didn't mind it.

"I suppose I did," he agreed.

"Drink?"

"That would be a pure pleasure, Sheriff."

"Rye all right?"

Longarm smiled. "A man after my own heart."

Dewar got a bottle out of the bottom file cabinet drawer, brought glasses out of a desk drawer, and poured for both of them. The rye was not a Maryland product, but it was mighty good.

"Thanks," Longarm said.

"This another of those courtesy calls, or is there something I should know about?" Dewar asked over the rim of his glass.

"Actually," Longarm said, "I was hoping to get some information from you."

"About a federal matter?"

"Yes. But I believe it may concern you too."

Dewar sat up straighter and looked interested. "Anything I can help you with, son. Just name it."

Longarm nodded. "That wire you sent me a while back. Said you were busy with a murder. Did you do any good?"

Dewar shook his head. "Not a damn bit of it," he said. He paused and smoothed his wide sweep of steel-gray moustache. "Not for lack of trying, either. I just can't get a thing on this one. A shot out of the dark. Like the night Wilse was shot. Except this one nobody wants to pretend was accidental. It bothers me, son."

"Your victim wouldn't happen to have been a man named Nagle, would it? Curtis Nagle?"

Dewar leaned forward abruptly. "Now how the hell would you know that?"

Longarm smiled and took another sip of his rye. "Oh, I was doing some reading, Sheriff. When I was trying to figure out who to tell about the accident down there at the mines." He paused. "You wouldn't have any more of this good stuff, would you?"

"Damn you, Long, you can have the whole bottle if you want. But what's this about Curt Nagle?"

Longarm helped himself to a refill and poured for Dewar as well. "Like I said, I was doing some reading. In a dead man's files. I found a few things, telegrams and letters, that I don't guess would've been left lying around if the owner of them hadn't already been dead."

"But . . ."

Longarm held a hand up. "I'm getting to it. Bear with me."

Dewar subsided, but reluctantly.

"It seems this Nagle was one of the principal stockholders in the Zuni Mountain Mining Company. So was another dead man, name of Wilse Howard. And it further seems that all the stock the both of those gentlemen controlled has now come under the ownership of a certain A. Howard of Gallup, New Mexico Territory. Interested?"

"Interested?" Dewar sputtered. "My God, son, you just give me motive for two murders if that's true."

178

"Oh, it's true enough." Longarm reached inside his coat and pulled out a folded sheaf of papers that he dropped on the desk in front of the sheriff.

"Those don't say . . . ?"

"Who did the murders?" Longarm shook his head. "Not exactly. It wasn't my man Bennett, I can tell you that much. I'm pretty sure Bennett killed Charles Carter, but he wasn't anywhere around Gallup when Howard and Nagle were killed. Besides, those papers are telling him about the deaths and the stock transfers. He obviously didn't do the killings or he wouldn't have had to be told that the victims were dead. The letters hint about things planned but not spelled out real clear. I was hoping you could make some sense out of that. Like whoever this A. Howard is. From the name I'd guess it to be, what, a son? brother? something like that?"

Dewar made a face. "Widow," he said.

"Mmm. Black widow."

"Black? No, son, she's a white woman."

Longarm smiled. "The black widow spider, Sheriff. The female kills and eats her mate after she's done with his usefulness."

"Oh. Yeah, that'd fit Alicia, all right. That's what the A. stands for. Alicia. Pretty as a new calf. Big eyes. Good ankles. Lot o' bosom."

"Steady hand?"

"I wouldn't know. She'd have to have a steady hand and a strong stomach if she was gonna murder her husband and his partner too." Dewar sighed. "Now all I got to do is prove this to a jury's satisfaction. Might not be so easy. Most juries aren't big on the idea of hanging women, you know."

"I'll leave that part of it to you. It isn't in my jurisdiction." Longarm smiled. "But there's another name in those papers that does come under my thumb. That one I'd kinda like to have for myself."

"Damn right you can have him, whoever he is. You sure helped me enough with this. Anything you want, Long, you just ask for it."

Longarm spoke the name, and Dewar lit up. "Why,

179

that's Alicia Howard's new fiancé," the sheriff said. "They just made the announcement. It isn't in the papers yet, but I heard it over lunch just today. It'll be printed in the next edition."

"If the editor is a friend of yours, Sheriff, I suggest you tell him to pull that story, then. The gentleman will be taking a ride with me, and I think it'll be a long time before he can come back here."

"You don't think he could've been the one pulling those triggers, do you?"

"Nope. He wasn't anywhere around here at the time of the first murder, and I doubt he'd have the nerve to have done the second if he was here then. Know where I can find him?"

"Of course. I'll take you there myself right now."

Longarm smiled and drained off the last of the good rye. Then he and Sheriff Dewar went out into the bright afternoon sunlight.

"Hello, Dalton."

Foster got red in the face and stood. "You! You can't do *anything* right."

Longarm laughed. "Messed up some big plans, didn't I, Dalton? Should I say I'm sorry about that? I'm not, you know." Longarm pulled out a cheroot, offered one to the sheriff, and then lighted both of them. He did not offer a smoke to Dalton Foster. "You know, Dalton, I was wondering why you wanted me on this Zuni case. I think I've figured it out. You thought this was one that couldn't be handled, and you just wanted a black mark on my record before you left the Bureau. Wasn't that it?"

Foster looked like he was going to bust.

"You don't know anything. You're guessing," he declared.

"Now you know me better than that, Dalton. I got everything I need, right down in black and white. You even signed one of those letters in your own hand. Not very smart, Dalton."

"You don't have . . ."

180

"I have enough to get you discharged from the Bureau and at least ten to fifteen years in the pokey, Dalton. Malfeasance, misfeasance, actions contrary to the interests of your wards . . . Shall I go on, Dalton?"

Foster withered, probably remembering some of the admissions he had made in the letter of instructions to Leon Bennett.

"It took me a while to figure some of it out, Dalton. Like why that wire was sent firing Charles Carter at that particular time. Bennett didn't know about Carter's plans to keep peace with the farmers. But you did. You were there that afternoon. And you just had time enough to race back here to Gallup and get Alicia Howard to fire Carter before a peaceful solution was reached. I wondered about that, Dalton. Then I figured you were greedy. You not only wanted the mine, you wanted that valley too. For what, Dalton? A land sales scheme? Run the Zuni and the Mexicans and the whites out and then you could take over their farms and sell them to somebody else as soon as the mine, your mine, quit deliberately causing the water problems? That sounds like you, Dalton. Greedy enough to have to grab with both hands." Longarm puffed on his smoke and stared at Foster.

"Straighten your back, darling. Haven't you any spine?" A tall, handsome woman wearing widow's weeds had swept into the room. Under other circumstances Longarm might have thought her attractive. At the moment, though, he saw her as a hard bitch.

Dalton Foster did not straighten his back. He continued to stare at the rose-patterned carpet in the Howard mansion.

"Sheriff," Alicia Howard said grandly. "And you, I presume, would be Marshal Long." She held her nose so high in the air she would drown in a good rain.

Dewar ignored her.

"You're under arrest, Dalton. You'll come with me to Denver for filing of the charges. Unless you want to resist arrest, that is. If you feel that lucky."

"Dalton!" The lady sounded shocked. "Sheriff Dewar, if

this man has done anything illegal, I assure you I didn't know about . . ."

"Shut your damn mouth, 'Licia," Dewar said. "You're next. I'll be back directly to arrest you for murder. You can think about that in the meantime."

Foster meekly shuffled forward and held his wrists out. Longarm obliged him with the handcuffs, then swiftly checked to make sure Foster was not armed. He was not.

"Sheriff. Really," Mrs. Howard protested. "You cannot possibly believe that I—"

"Eat a good supper tonight, 'Licia. You might not like what we serve in the jail. And I suggest you bathe good too. No telling what you might pick up from the drunken squaws and hoors you'll be sharing your cell with."

Mrs. Howard paled and began to wring her hands.

Longarm led Foster outside, Dewar following. "A little hard on her, weren't you?" he asked when they were out of hearing.

Dewar smiled. "Curt Nagle was a good friend of mine, Long. In fact, I think you met him. He was in the office that first time you called."

Longarm remembered him now. They had not actually been introduced at the time.

"What I'm really hoping, o' course," Dewar admitted, "is that the widow woman will save the taxpayers and good voters of this community the expense of taking her to a trial we likely wouldn't win anyway. With luck she'll suicide out before I come back to fetch her."

"And if she doesn't?"

Dewar smiled. "I'll think of something," he assured the younger officer.

Interesting way they had of enforcing the laws hereabouts, Longarm thought. But not his problem and not his jurisdiction. "I'll be needing to borrow a couple of those letters to use as evidence against Foster," he said.

"Anything you want, son. Always glad to lend a hand."

Dalton Foster acted as though he had not heard.

"Tell you what, Long. Let's park that prisoner of yours

in my jail, and I'll treat you to the finest cooking this side of Kansas City. Are you game?"

"My pleasure, Sheriff."

Dalton Foster shambled along beside them like a sleepwalker. It was going to be a long and lonely ride back to Denver, Longarm thought. But satisfying.

Watch for

LONGARM AND THE BLOODY TRACKDOWN

one hundred and ninth novel in the bold
LONGARM series from Jove

coming in January!